Charlotte Armst
attended the Univ
Barnard College
      After graduatio.

ing operator for *The New York Times,* a fashion reporter for a buyer's guide, and an office worker for a firm of accountants. During this time, she also sold several poems to *The New Yorker.* In 1928 she married Jack Lewi, an advertising executive.

After her marriage, Miss Armstrong's interest turned to writing plays, two of which were produced on Broadway. Neither was successful, but during rehearsals for her second play, her first novel, a mystery entitled *Lay On, MacDuff,* was published. She had found her metier.

Eventually, the Lewis moved to Southern California, which became the setting of much of her later work. In 1956 Charlotte Armstrong won the Mystery Writers of America's best novel award for *A Dram of Poison.* In 1957 her fellow Californian, the great mystery critic Anthony Boucher, wrote in his column in *The New York Times Book Review:* "The festival of Halloween ten days ago was, I trust, celebrated with peculiarly fitting rites in Glendale, Calif.; for there dwells one of the few authentic spellcasting witches of modern times: Charlotte Armstrong."

Miss Armstrong also wrote the screen adaptations of two of her novels. *The Unsuspected* starred Claude Raines. *Don't Bother to Knock,* the film version of *Mischief,* featured Marilyn Monroe in her first starring role along with Richard Widmark and Anne Bancroft.

Until her sadly premature death in 1969, Charlotte Armstrong wrote 27 novels, all in the mystery/suspense genre, many of them classics. Library of Crime Classics editor-in-chief Burke N. Hare has hailed Miss Armstrong as "the finest American novelist of suspense of the twentieth century."

CHARLOTTE ARMSTRONG
available from IPL Library of Crime Classics®

CHARLOTTE ARMSTRONG

THE WITCH'S HOUSE

LIBRARY OF CRIME CLASSICS ®

MISTER E'S ™

INTERNATIONAL POLYGONICS, LTD.
NEW YORK CITY

THE WITCH'S HOUSE

Library of Congress Card Catalog No. 90-84277
ISBN 1-55882-081-7

Printed and manufactured in the United States of America.
First IPL printing January 1991.
10 9 8 7 6 5 4 3 2 1

To A. B.

Monday

He happened to be standing perfectly still, considering what, if anything, he ought to take home. Papers to grade? Class statistics to bring up to date? He was a young mathematics instructor named Elihu (but mercifully nicknamed Pat) O'Shea; he was accustomed to using his mind and not his fingers. Therefore, he did not paw his desk or flip his calendar, but, standing still, he marshaled and reviewed his obligations.

His cubicle, all done in gray metal and something less than cozy, looked east; it was dim, at this hour in early March. When the door of the office directly across the corridor opened, the band of late sunlight did not reach all the way to Pat's open door. Pat could physically see his fellow faculty member, Professor Everett Adams (Biology) also preparing to leave at the end of Monday, but Everett did not notice him, and Pat did not move or speak. He was no pal of Everett's, whom he considered a dull old bunny. Nor did he think about the other man, particularly, until sight suddenly connected with brain, and Pat came to startled attention.

Everett Adams was a pace within his own place. No one else could see him at all as he took an object out of his right-hand jacket pocket, transferred it to his left and adjusted his left arm, and the briefcase it held, so as to minimize the bulge of the object. Then Everett stepped into the corridor, pulled his door shut, and locked it.

A sound came out of Pat O'Shea, a growl of angry astonishment. Everett swiveled his thatch of gray. He had very large brown eyes, set abnormally far apart, so that his temples looked thin and flat. The eyes flashed, seeming to reveal a moment of anguished shock. Then they veiled themselves. Everett hunched his narrow shoulders and strode off.

Pat O'Shea yanked open his top desk drawer, swept papers within, shut it, locked it, snatched his brown raincoat from the gray metal clothes tree, and whirled out of his office.

He was furious! *So?* But was it so?

Everett, scurrying toward the intersecting corridor, was detouring now around a knot of students in front of a bulletin board. Pat went after him. When he was angry, his amiable rugged face became another face. Now, as he walked fast, just without running, one of the students detached himself from the group to stare curiously at him. Pat checked himself.

If he had seen what he thought he had seen, *then* he was very angry indeed. But could he be absolutely sure? No. So he would not run, shout, or make a fuss. And he had better not let this particular student suspect that anything was up.

This Parsons boy was neither an athlete nor a brain and not gifted with any particular charm. Nevertheless, he had constituted himself the college gossip and, as such, he had power. It was best not to stir him up, because he was not scrupulous about what tales he told, but relished the exercise of his imagination, in which might lie all the power Mike Parsons would ever have. So Pat slowed down, dismissed as best he could the black look that anger put on his face, murmured a hail and farewell, and strolled by, knowing that Everett Adams had made it to the next wing, down which he would go to the left where, at the end, a flight of stairs led to a lower-level exit to the faculty parking lot. This was Pat's own natural route and he pursued it.

At the intersection of corridors, there was a glass-enclosed place where Joanne Knowles was on the department switchboard. Turning the corner, Pat waved to her, since she was supposed to know what faculty members were in or not in the Science Building. Then he drove his long legs to go faster than he appeared to be going.

Ahead of him, and moving fast, Everett Adams ducked downward. Pat reached the stairs and went bonging down their metal treads. Everett was at the door, at the bottom. Pat hit the glass while it still swung and as he came out into the shaded spot, he shouted, "Adams!"

But Everett was into his car, a 1960 Chevrolet Bel Air, and putting it into motion very quickly. Pat was just leaping down the two broad stone steps to the pavement when Everett backed out of his slot, reversed, and went sailing away. As he did so Pat saw a form, draped in flowered cotton, rise from the coping of a low stone wall that held back the plantings across this sunken court. But he was running to his own '61 tan Rambler, and he pretended not to see the girl, although he knew, at once, who she was and why she was there. She was Vee Adams, Everett's daughter, and she must have been waiting, over there on the sunny side, to ride home with her father.

But Everett had "forgotten" her. Oh-ho, had he, though?

Guilty, thought Pat. By golly, he *is* guilty and he knows I know it. So Pat felt furious all over again.

It certainly looked as if the thing in Everett's jacket pocket was that ultraviolet-reflecting objective for a microscope, an attachment so delicate and fine as to be very expensive, indeed. Just such a small precious piece of laboratory equipment had disappeared, ten days ago, from the University's Science Building. Presumed stolen.

What was making Pat O'Shea so furious was the fact that although there was no proof of the thief's identity, and no open accusation, nevertheless there was suspicion. And the continuance in the University of a second-year student named Rossi was being made not only miserable, but almost impossible. He was the only student known to have been alone in the laboratory on the morning the theft had been discovered. Only that. But it was enough.

This Rossi was a boy whom Pat had wished to encourage. Pat had wanted him to believe that he was free to move from the background of his kin to the company of his kind. The boy came of uneducated people who did not fully understand his urge toward knowledge, but the boy had the qualities that lift a teacher's tired heart. How could the poor kid keep his mind on his studies, or believe in his opportunity, in the shadow of this doubt, so cruel—if he were innocent?

Now, if this . . . this . . . this . . . (Pat couldn't find a word dirty enough for Everett Adams) . . . this highly respected, pompous old *bunny*—who had even called a meeting and spoken high-minded words about basic honesty—if he himself was just now making off with the *loot* . . . !

The man must be crazy! But, crazy or not, Everett Adams wasn't going to watch, from his cozy burrow of privilege, a valuable boy's life-chance snuff out. Not now. Not if Pat had seen what he thought he had seen. Pat would take care of that. *If.* So Pat's car jumped.

Everett had not turned upgrade, to his right, toward the Main Gate as he normally would, but to his left. O.K., thought Pat, suddenly jubilant. Follow that car! Wherever the dickens Everett thought he was going, Pat O'Shea was going too. He intended to catch up with and confront the man while the thing was still in his pocket. If the thing was Everett's property, Pat could apologize. Natural mistake. So sorry. But he would have to find out.

And he thought he would find out. After all, the driver ahead could hardly throw a thing out of the car without the driver behind detecting such a movement. And if Everett dropped it quietly overboard, Pat would see it hit the road. Oh no, no, Everett was not going to get away with a thing. Pat turned gleefully left, to follow.

Strict rules prevailed against speed on the campus so the two cars proceeded with dignified obedience past the Library and the Administration Building and bent away to go around the gymnasium, past the tennis courts, to an exit at the southwest corner of the campus. Here, where Everett might have turned left to regain the main road into town, again he chose the other way.

Pat nosed into traffic behind him. This street pertained to nothing significant that he could imagine but, about a mile farther on, it would cross another popular route into the heart of the town. Pat trundled along behind, angry, but holding to the fair doubt, knowing very well that "to see something with your own eyes" is not always reliable evidence.

At the junction, Everett did not turn toward town but to his right, which way would lead him out into the country. Pat, suddenly impatient, came up to the intersection rapping his horn button, in the swift *toot-toot-toot* which means "Give me your attention. I want to speak to you." Everett must have heard it, but he did not even hesitate. On the contrary, his car picked up its heels.

Pat whipped around the corner in his wake, thinking, Guilty, all right! The guilty flee and I pursueth.

(There was a gas station on that corner. Far in upon the concrete, a lad named Dick Green was hosing off a car. He looked up, at the horn blasts, and saw Mr. O'Shea, from whom he took calculus at the University. Dick half raised a hand in greeting. But Mr. O'Shea had not seen him—just went busting around the corner. Funny.)

Now, they were going north and it was becoming country. Pat did not attempt to speed and pass and block Everett's way. Dangerous and unnecessary. Wherever he can go, I can go, Pat thought, and when he stops, there I'll be. His nemesis is what I am. He grinned to himself, thinking how he would tell Anabel about this cops-and-robbers adventure. The street had become a highway which ran straight. There was home-going traffic on it, but Pat hung on the Chevy's heels. Let the guilty suffer.

Up ahead, a red light bloomed. As Everett slid up to the stop, four cars were already motionless there. Everett, with Pat behind him, was in the middle lane. To their left, the left-turn slot was being entered by the car behind them.

Everett suddenly yanked his wheel, nipped around the cars that waited, flashed through the left-turn slot, and ran the light. The car entering the slot squealed and braked, and hemmed Pat in.

Well, well, well! Pat rolled to his own legal position and stopped there. Everything he does says he's guilty, the fool! Or why does he run away from me? Which he has just successfully done, by the way. O.K. Even so. All *I* have to do is turn the suspicion on him, which I can do with many hedges, from a position of noble doubt and humility before the truth, and so on . . . and he will have had it. And Rossi will be all right. So . . . why don't I just go on home?

But Pat didn't want to go on home. He was not only furious about the theft, the injustice, but miffed on his own account. He had been tricked, caught napping, and he didn't like it. Furthermore, the position of noble doubt and humble inquiry did not fall in anything like as well with his mood, as to catch Everett personally and tell him a thing or two. Right now.

But Everett's car had slipped over a small rise, and Pat was stuck here.

When the light changed, Pat came up over the rise, surveyed the scene and saw, a mile away, perhaps, the right-turn blinker of some car, flashing. But it was only a glimpse. The road was streaming. The moving ribbons were multicolored. He could not spot the blue Chevy. He began to work his way into the right lane and look for a place to stop a moment. Think a moment. Have some sense, maybe.

By the time he had switched lanes he was nearly upon a side road. On the near corner there was a little grocery store which displayed the sign of the bell. Then he must stop here, use the public phone and call Anabel. Pat would normally have been home five or ten minutes ago. It would take a good while to get back to town, and then on home, from where he was now. He would be very late. Better call. Confess this chase and his defeat. Well? Pat turned into the side road, whose sign read OLEANDER STREET. A delivery boy was busily backing his panel truck into a slot behind the grocery store.

Pat called out, on impulse, "Hey, did a car turn in here just now?"

"What's that?" The boy had a red head, a long thin freckled nose, and a stupefied expression.

Pat repeated his question and the boy said, "Sure did. And left rubber." He began to look interested. "Can I do anything—"

"Was it a Chevy? Blue?"

"It was blue. I'll tell you that much. But see, I was watching my left rear—"

"Where does this road lead?"

"No place."

"Dead end, you mean?"

"That's right."

"Any crossroads?"

"Nope. Not one."

"Oh," said Pat. "Thanks a lot."

"You bet," said the grocery boy.

Pat stepped on the gas joyfully. If a car, a *blue* car, had squealed around this corner, it might very well have been Everett, who was in a hurry all right. Pat had seen a signal blinking. By golly, from habit—and law-abiding habit, at that—had the fox signaled the hound? If so, if so, then

Everett was trapped on a dead-end street with no cross-roads, *Get him yet,* Pat thought.

Oleander Street was paved, but narrow and meandering. Far ahead rose some of Southern California's sudden hills, barren and dry, uninhabited. Oleander Street would not lead up into them. It twisted along the level, no thorough-fare, simply an access road for the small truck farms that were hardly more than garden patches, and the small chicken "ranches" that were staggered along on either side, each with its small house, erratically placed.

What was Everett Adams doing here? *If* here.

Proceeding slowly, now, and watching on all sides for any glimpse of the car he hunted, Pat came drifting around a curve and stopped, because there was a knot of chattering people in the road. He was directly opposite a picket gate, beside which there stood a wooden platform about four feet high on which there had been bolted a wooden armchair. Pat looked at this structure and saw a boy, about nine years old, sitting in the elevated chair with his thin unevenly de-veloped legs stretched before him in their metal braces. Pat felt a quick pang for whatever father had built this con-traption.

But the little boy was not having anybody's pity. His big brown eyes were blazing. "Mister? Mister?"

"What happened, old-timer?" Pat leaned out.

"A hit and run! A killer!" shouted the little boy. "Killed my mother's chicken. Didn't stop!"

"What kind of car?"

"Blue, 1960, Bel Air," shouted the boy with the sure knowledge of little boys. "Four-door, two-tone, didn't get the license. Sticker on the rear window, yellow and blue—"

"Right you are," Pat said. (The University's parking stickers were yellow and blue.) "Where did he go?"

The boy pointed on along Oleander.

"This street goes where?"

"Nowhere," cried the boy. "Just to the witch's. Catch him, mister. Please catch him?" He leaned out of the chair almost to the point of falling. "Take me."

"I'll catch him," said Pat, cheerfully. "You sit tight."

He saluted and let the car move gently. The half-dozen women and children did not speak to him. Now he could see the mangled bird, a patch of blood and feathers, and he was careful to avoid it. In his rearview mirror, he saw the people beginning to disperse.

Jamie Montero's mother lifted her son down from his perch. Jamie cried, "No, Mama. No, Mama. Wait, Mama. He is going to catch the killer. The nice man! Mama, the bad man killed your chicken and he didn't stop. But the nice man will catch him."

"Hush-hush-hush," his mother said. "Suppertime. Hush, we are rich. It don't bother us that much."

Pat went, warily, farther along the meandering road. He had not caught the word the boy had used. *Just to the . . .* WHAT? No matter. The houses were thinning. Not far ahead, the terrain was beginning to roughen. On this flat land there were a few live oaks, a stand of lemon eucalyptus ahead, and one square of darker trees over there, which usually meant that someone had planted them. Was there one more house, within that square?

Ah now—the final curve to the right and suddenly, on a fan-shaped flat of dust, the end of the road.

Within the trees directly ahead of him there was, indeed,

a dilapidated old California bungalow, gray from the weather—a slightly crooked house within a crooked fence. There was no garage, no driveway. But to his left, where the eucalyptus grove stood, Pat could see in the waning light far in among the barkless trunks a glimpse of blue. A car.

He cut his motor, set his brake, and stepped out.

Got him! Pat thought.

Everett Adams leaned over the brink, staring down at the heap of trash. This arroyo was, or had been, an unauthorized dump, used by those who wanted to be rid of garden clippings without paying the fee at the legal place. Everett had gardened for fun in other days, long ago, when Lillian was alive. Since then, the city fathers had posted the place. The heaps below were moldering. Everett was running his straining gaze over the humps and surfaces to be sure the bright metal that he had just cast over had gone deep enough into the confusion.

He was thinking, Damn O'Shea, never closes his door! Didn't occur to me . . . What did he see? Foolish to panic. Could have simply stared him down. Or could have said, "I did it for money." They'd boot me out. Twenty years of teaching. Ah, but the risk . . . No. Let it alone now. Shaken him off. Rid of it. No one will ever know. . . .

He felt sick. He was a sick man. His brain flipped and flopped and flubbed. He looked behind him and saw O'Shea's figure coming, in the greenish gloom, between the slim and pale and naked trunks of the trees. The short twilight seemed upon them. The sky was strange. The light was yellow-green and O'Shea's figure, a bright gray, came on, not fast but steadily. It was like doom.

Everett took four steps to his car. O'Shea didn't understand. Didn't know. Even if he knew, would he understand? No, no, the risk . . . Stare him down.

"Are you following me, O'Shea?" he cried out angrily. "May I ask what the idea is?"

O'Shea kept coming. "May I ask what you've got in your pocket?" He was cold, hard. He was doom.

"I beg your pardon?" Everett pulled in his chin, tried to look haughtily outraged, but he had to keep his hand on the sill of the open door of his car to steady his knees.

O'Shea seemed to study the hang of his jacket. Then O'Shea walked to the brink and glanced over. "I see," he said contemptuously. "Got rid of it, did you?"

Everett stood and strove to hide his trembling. Even the car trembled. He hadn't cut his motor, that was it. He licked his mouth and tried for words appropriate to outraged innocence. He couldn't think. Flip, flop, flub . . . Rage took him and its strength shook him and he shouted, "No, you don't see! I'm trying to save a human soul. You wouldn't understand that. You don't know and you don't see . . ."

O'Shea wasn't even listening. He began to shout. "Look out, you idiot!"

Everett was forced to stagger because his car was moving. It crept. It was too close to the brink. What was happening must not happen. He threw his weight against the door, grasping the metal with both hands. The car was gaining momentum. He should have tried to get around and at the brakes. His feet were slipping.

Then O'Shea's hard hands grabbed him and pulled at him and Everett was torn away to fall on the ground, all tangled with O'Shea, and from there to see his car go down with a crunch as its front wheels slid over the edge. It slid another foot or two. Then it lifted its hindquarters slowly up, it tottered, it slid again. It described a stately, fated, heels-over-head, down into the arroyo.

O'Shea was making a moaning sound. Everett himself was crying, in high-pitched squeals, from far up in the middle of his skull. Neither could rise nor run nor see over. They caught breath, with a single impulse to listen. Nothing came to their ears. No explosion. Not even engine sound. Nor to their eyes any gush of black smoke and hot flame out of the gulch. Everett's car had simply disappeared.

Everett squirmed and ground one knee into the slippery leaf-strewn soil. He turned his furious face downward. "Now you did it! Now everything is going to happen. You wouldn't wait! You wouldn't listen! You wouldn't even try to understand!"

O'Shea lay on his back with his face white. He said quietly, "I think my ankle or my leg is busted."

"Good!" cried Everett, frothing. "Good! Because by what right do *you* judge? By what self-righteous ignorance do *you* destroy?"

It didn't occur to him that he might have gone over the brink and been crushed himself, or that O'Shea had been trying to save his life. He thought he had been attacked. Into his mind were sifting patchy visions of the consequences. Never get the car out without a crane. Without people, who would find out. Couldn't lose a car and say nothing. It would be found. And prove to be his. Ought to have burned. No, fire would have brought people. But there were no people here . . . not yet.

Suppose the car were never found? Or, he could say it

had been stolen. Ah no, stupid! Here was O'Shea, to tell the whole story. And the stolen object would be found, too, because O'Shea knew it was there.

Damn O'Shea!

"Oh, damn you!" croaked Everett. "You know absolutely nothing about the real problem. You think it matters to me anymore? You think it weighs in the scale against a human soul?" A final outrage. O'Shea wasn't even listening now. In O'Shea's eyes, Everett read himself dismissed as incomprehensible. As probably quite mad. So Everett's right hand found a stone. His right hand went high, of itself. O'Shea jerked his head but the stone came crashing down. The head turned bloody at the side. Very bloody. Everett raised the stone again. Had to finish it now. A point of no return. No other way. He brought the stone down a second time.

His arm went weak. All his limbs turned soft. He began to pant—great gasps for air that were like sobs. O'Shea was out of it. Bloody, limp, and silent upon the ground. O'Shea was dead.

Well, then, at least he couldn't tell.

Everett's breath sawed. He got to his feet and staggered to the brink. The drop-over was twenty-five or thirty feet. There lay his car, upside down, on a slant, helpless as a turtle, its wheels still turning. But no sound. The motor had stalled? Or what? No matter. Nothing could be done about the car.

What could be done at all? At all? Now he had sacrificed, indeed. Must this, too, be for nothing? Tried to think.

Could he switch the story around, say it was O'Shea who had the stolen thing and Everett who had pursued him and here, at the end of the road, fought with a criminal at bay? In self-defense? Did Everett have the cold nerve to tell that story and keep to it? No, no, impossible. The cars in themselves told the order of their going. Or someone must have seen them, along the way. The pursuer doesn't go first. No, *think*.

Hide the body? He had an instinct to hide the body, put it over the brink into the dump and simply leave it. And go home. Say that his car had been stolen. Know nothing.

But how to go home or even back into town? Why, in O'Shea's car, of course. Get away from here. Keys? Everett went down on one knee and began to pry into O'Shea's pockets. Eyes shut. Fingers would do. Couldn't look. No keys?

Everett turned his back and bent to weep. He couldn't. He was finished. It was all over, all up with her, and with him too. He'd never meant to come to this. All so stupid, so incredibly stupid. And so inevitable.

Kneeling in the grove, with the dark thickening, Everett could feel a cool trickle of truth seeping into his understanding. He had been dominated for a long time by something that had simply wiped out his intelligence. Now, he was destroyed.

But as he knelt there, the oldest instinct stirred and it was cool, like truth. Run, then.

Maybe the keys were in the car. Money? He walked on his knees, he pushed at the limpness, got O'Shea's wallet. Take it. Too late for scruples. A long time too late. He had sacrificed them. *Now*, should he hide the body? Yes, of course, hide it. Smooth out the tracks, the gashes in the ground. Bury the blood. Confuse the signs. Run. Hide.

And give her up—which was the one thing demanded of him from the beginning. Now he could see clearly that it was accomplished.

He rose. His breath was coming more slowly. There was something of comfort, something almost delicious, about having it all over. So to simplicity. To eat, to drink, to sleep, and rise again to eat, to drink . . . A dog was barking.

Everett tingled with the shock. No, no, he had to think this out. Had to have more time. Could not be caught now and taken, irrevocably, to the drama of cops and courts and fame and shame. Not before he had thought!

His trouser knees were stained with dirt. He had O'Shea's wallet in his hand. He put his head down and went stumbling and sometimes sliding to O'Shea's Rambler. He had the terror of the hunted on him, already. But the keys were in the car. An omen, surely! Everett got in and started the motor.

He didn't have to reverse, he could circle here. He circled, holding the wheel as far as he could to the left with a suspicion that he could never move it again, that he would just go around and around and around until the gasoline was gone. It had become very dark. The sky rumbled Storm? Well, yes, the weather report . . . That yellowish light had been warning. The car had come around half circle. His mind was going around again. Everett bit his teeth together and wrenched at the wheel. The car bounced upon Oleander Street's worn pavement.

Headlights? Fumbling for the switch, his icy fingers found it. He was really quite clever. But what was behind?

He looked into the rearview mirror. All he could see, against what light there was left in the sky, were the moving trunks of the trees as they swished their tall tops in a sudden wind. Then lightning flashed and in the flash Everett saw behind him the figure of a woman, all in black, and he saw beside her a huge black dog.

The fiend: it was the fiend!

He shuddered, head to toe. His toe shook on the accelerator. He made the curve. His scalp crept. The sky cracked.

When the sky cracked, it was as if the film had been jolted back upon the sprockets; the pictures of consciousness began to run in Pat's mind. His lids lifted to a darkish world. He could hear, he could sense, the beast coming. He could smell, he could feel, the breath upon his skin, the snuffling; the muttering threat in the throat was loud to him.

"Nice doggie?" Pat murmured. His head shifted; the pain cracked. Light flashed and went out.

The sound of thunder roused Anabel O'Shea from her book. Ah, the predicted storm. Listening, she could hear no tinny drumming sound where the house gutter ought to have been fixed. Not raining yet, then. Pat had his raincoat. She had reminded him.

But, sitting in her favorite corner of the living room, she felt uneasy. Why? All her duties had been done, little Sue abed, dinner ready—"held back" in the oven—table set, house and herself neatened, the whole ménage ready for Pat to come home. She must feel guilty for having been reading so long, going with the novel, absorbed by the characters. Was it so long?

She looked at the time. Pat was a little late, but half an hour was nothing. He would come in a minute.

Anabel chewed her lip. Had she apologized? Yes, as she

remembered they had both apologized—well enough. Pat for making the date with the Provost and his wife for some stupid party on Saturday night when Anabel had wanted to go to the concert. And Anabel for blowing off almost all of her disappointment and disapproval. She had a temper; this was understood by both of them. Yes, they had given each other the pecks and the pats that signified "I'll get over it." And Anabel had sputtered around the house for twenty minutes more and then had been over it. Hadn't given it another thought, until now.

It wasn't worth another thought. She got up and went around to all the windows. It was going to rain and she might as well batten down the hatches. When she had made the complete round of their neat modern house, all on one floor and on its way to being furnished, although still on the bare side, Anabel worried briefly for the seeds she had put in hopefully along the garden wall. Rain would be wonderful—if it didn't wash them out. Anabel liked her house and garden very much and was in the midst of many projects. Why didn't Pat come?

She sighed and loosened her shoulders, took a couple of dance steps, considered music. But she did not turn on the FM. She went back to her chair and her book, wishing, for some reason, to keep her ear on the state of the universe.

The book was losing her or she was losing the book. She kept listening for the car, for the phone, for the rain.

At a quarter of seven, she leaped up, ran to the kitchen and turned everything all the way off. Dinner wasn't going to be very good, she thought ruefully.

Then, moving slowly on her long handsome legs, holding her honey-colored head to one side, pushing her lower lip out in the expression of the stubborn child who "doesn't care," Anabel went to the phone and dialed the University's number. No answer. She dialed the night number, asked to be connected with Pat's extension. No answer. Anabel hung up and scolded herself for such female carryings-on as this. But it was seven o'clock, so she found and dialed another number.

"Joanne? This is Anabel O'Shea."

"Oh, hi."

"Say, did Pat leave late, or something, do you know?"

"He left about his usual time," said Joanne Knowles. "Why, Anabel?"

"Well, he hasn't gotten here and I'm wondering what to do with some pretty sad-looking lamb chops."

"But it's after seven!"

"That's what I mean. Well, he's been detained someplace, that's all. I didn't know but what the Provost had everybody locked up in a meeting, and Pat was stuck."

"No, no. He left . . . it must have been just a bit after five-thirty. I'm sorry I can't tell you anything more. I'm sorry if you're worried," worried Joanne.

"Oh, I'm not, really. Just wondering." Anabel chatted a few minutes more. When she hung up she heard the rain beginning.

The storm had been a long time breaking, but when it broke it was a deluge. The drumming of the drops lasted only a moment. Then the rain fell in a solid, relentlessly total rush. "Wow!" said Anabel aloud.

She moved the draperies in the living room. Even the streetlights were nothing but a yellow shimmer behind silver. Nobody could drive in this. Wherever Pat was, he would have to stay, now, and wait this out. No use expecting him. He could not come in this rain. The house felt like a locked box, shut up to only its own supply of air. It was hard to breathe. Anabel hoped that Sue, who was only four, wouldn't wake up and be frightened. There was nothing to be afraid of, was there?

The rain fell on the plain and on the mountains.

Partway up the mountain, within the pass, there was a diner, a place called Hamburger Haven. Ten minutes after the storm began, the place was packed. For one thing, a transcontinental bus driver had come early, thankfully shepherding his flock. Then one motorist after another had crept gratefully off the road into the parking space and he, and whatever passengers he carried, had come running through the wall of water. Now the place steamed with damp people, and the help scurried desperately to serve everyone, for people were stimulated to great hunger and thirst by the adventure of it. But they were genial and patient with each other, safe here from the weather and all of them, in a manner of speaking, in the same boat. They were noisy. Hamburger Haven was doing a business that literally roared.

When the rain had been coming down some twenty-five minutes, the door opened once more. "Mule" Mueller, behind the counter, saw a plump man, dashing water from his hat brim, zigzagging between groups of people, talking to himself.

He reached the counter and a customer moved obligingly to give the newcomer room. "Great night for ducks, eh?" said this customer.

"I dunno how we ever made it," said the plump man

earnestly, fearfully, triumphantly. "I tell you, it's a miracle. Got a cup of coffee there, Mac? What'll *you* have?"

The plump man's head turned far to his left and slowly his whole torso began to twist left. Then he turned back and said to Mule, "Where's the fellow that came in with me?"

Mule shook his head slightly.

"Wait a minute," said the plump one. "You saw us come in."

"Saw *you*, mister."

"Huh?" The plump one pulled away from the counter and went weaving his way back to the door. Mule had a few floodlights out there, but they were helpless. The plump man opened the door and peered out. There was just this silver brightness. He stood there in the open door, a fine mist blowing in past him, until somebody shouted, "Hey, shut the door. Do you mind?"

Whereupon, the plump man shut the door. He came back to the counter and leaned upon it heavily. Damp and pale.

"Coffee, you said?" Mule inquired.

"Right. Yeah. Thanks."

The plump man's excitement had leaked out of him entirely. He was silent and subdued. He rubbed his chin, his cheeks. He took off his glasses suddenly and rubbed his eyes with stiff fingers.

The rain roared upon the old roof and it rushed down all around. Within the room, dust seemed to be shaken out of the walls and ceiling. The place was dry and dusty. Pat O'Shea blamed his own senses, at first. He thought the roaring was in his own head and the acrid air a dryness in his own nostrils.

He knew that he was hurt. When he tried to open his eyes his head ached violently. There was light from some source, here where he was, and the light hit his pupils like a knife cut. So he held his lids against pain and tried to guess where he was. He was lying on something soft and he was covered. He could listen. . . .

"Ah, now. Ah, now. They couldn't and I knew they couldn't. Never, never keep him. Not Johnny Pryde. Eh, Rex? Eh? Eh?"

A woman's voice, was it? A dog barked. Not loudly. It was just as if the dog had understood her words and was answering them. The dog was saying "That's right."

The woman said, "That's right. Johnny's home. Eh, Rex? Ah, now. Johnny Pryde. Them cops, never going to get you. Not you. No more. No fear," she said.

Pat forced his eyes open. He was lying on a bed, an old-fashioned double bed with a high carved wooden headboard curving above him. The room was very small and perfectly square. It was wallpapered; the paper was much faded. There was a chest of drawers, a wooden chair, a small table with a marble top, and one lamp burning. It really was a lamp, with a wick, burning.

All this Pat saw but did not even list in his mind yet, because he was looking at the old woman in the black dress.

Her hair was white and cut in short wild locks that rumbled in confusion on her head. Her eyes were black and bright. Her face was seamed with a thousand wrinkles and it was the color of a brown eggshell. Her lips had a blue and gummy look. She was thin, bent. She had a staff in her hand—a stout stick it was, but straight and much handled, as smooth as if it had been polished. Her hands were claws and they were folded around the staff.

Now she began to laugh. A cackling sound, with a small shriek running in and out of the sound to give an effect of high and malicious glee. "You're home," she cackled. "Johnny Pryde."

Pat put aside the consideration of his injuries and swallowed hard. He lifted himself on an elbow. "What happened?"

"I knew you'd come home. I've been waiting. Me and Rex. Waiting a long time. But we knew. Eh, Rex?"

The dog answered. Pat's startled eyes saw the black fierce head, the teeth, the dog's lip beginning to curl.

"Good dog. Good Rex. Here's Johnny. Good Johnny. Mind, Rex." The old woman's voice became sharp. "Go, Rex. Guard. Guard the door."

The dog protested, in a small mutter, but then it obeyed. It turned away and padded into another room.

Pat had caught his lower lip in his teeth. Now he released it. "I'm glad you speak his language," he said. "Have you a telephone, ma'am?"

"No fear," she said. "Nobody'll get you now. Never. No more."

Pat shut his eyes, because the light hurt so much. He cleared his throat. "My name is O'Shea," he said politely. "I teach at the University. I've had a little trouble, it seems. What time is it?" He knew he could not focus on his watch. "Could you please call my wife?"

He began to struggle to sit higher up against the headboard. She came to help him. Her old hands were hard and strong. She put them under his arms and helped him. But now there was a drag upon his right foot and Pat clenched his teeth.

He remembered his knowledge of something breaking when he fell with Everett Adams. He remembered, and saw in a vision upon his eyelids, that face in an extremity of rage and fear.

"My leg . . ." he began.

"Never go back there. Never. No more," the old woman was crooning. "You've come home and I'll take care. No fear."

"I'm very sorry," Pat said, tightening against pain, opening his eyes. The long staff had fallen against her shoulder and she was holding it with her chin. Her black eyes were shining. "But I am not anybody named Johnny, ma'am," Pat went on. "My name is O'Shea. I am a teacher at the University. If you have a telephone, would you please call . . . What's the time?" Now he felt anxious. "Anabel will be worried sick."

"Ah, now," the old woman said, "nobody bothers me. You'll see, Johnny Pryde." She put her hands on her staff and the end of it against her leathery cheek.

He thought, Where's her hat? She was almost comically the witch in the fairy tales. She lacked only the high black conical hat. And the cat. Pat caught his mind slipping off toward nonsense. "What goes on here?" he muttered, and began to shift his legs.

Something pretty drastic was wrong with his right leg, just above the anklebone. He wasn't sure that he could walk, but he could hop, he supposed. Now he realized that the continuing rush and roar was out-of-doors. "Is that rain?" he exclaimed.

"Rain," said the old woman. "Good rain. You remember Pa putting the new roof on? You was too little, Johnny? Your grandpa, he didn't want it, but your pa, he put the good roof on and no rain gets in. No more. No more."

Pat squinted at her and said, "Mrs. Whatever-your-name-is, I am grateful to you for bringing me in out of the rain. But I have to get back to town and to my wife and little girl. So if you please—"

"No girls," she said severely. "None of them. None of them. Them girls, them damned mean and sneaking, lying girls. I knew they was lying. I knew it. And I knew you'd come home, Johnny Pryde, and no girls. No more. No more."

"Ma'am," said Pat grimly, "if you don't mind, please try to stop talking like Poe's raven. . . ." He was not quite fully aware of the almost total lack of communication here. He had a notion that the old woman was deaf. Then he must speak slowly and with more volume, and be very patient. Straining to be loud and clear, he said, "Help me to your telephone."

"No telephone," she answered.

"Neighbors?"

"No neighbors. You'll see, Johnny Pryde." She cackled, suddenly.

"Then, will you please . . ." Pat leaned back. Not in this rain. She couldn't go anywhere to get help until the cloudburst was over. Pat felt confused. He murmured, "How long has it been raining like this? How long was I out, anyway?"

"Ten years," she said. "Ten, pretty near eleven. But I knew. *They* couldn't keep you. I knew you'd come. I waited. Didn't I? But no more."

She wasn't deaf. Pat thought, Then she's mad as a hatter. He let himself back against the pillow. He moved his right foot and the pain stabbed. He looked at his right hand. It was scraped and lacerated and something had punctured it, deep, there along the edge of his palm. The wounds were dirty. He put his left hand to his head. The left side of his head was encrusted with a dried something. Could it be blood? He said, "I think I'd better get to a doctor."

"No doctor," she said. "Nobody. I'll take care. I know more than them doctors. None of them."

"Can you boil some water?" he snapped. "I'd like to be clean."

Her black eyes sparkled. "I brought water." Letting the staff lean on the wall, she turned to the marble-topped table and he saw that there was a crockery bowl on it and an old rag that she picked up in her claws. She dipped the rag. She wrung it out.

He said, sharply, "Let me see that."

But she was leaning very close now. He could smell something sourish. She began to mop gently at the side of his head with the wet rag, which was cold. He winced away. "Let that alone, please. Never mind. It's my leg. May need setting."

"I know what to do," she said. "No fear." Her eyes shone. Pat realized that she was happy and that this was very frightening to him. He didn't yet understand why.

She pulled the blanket away from his body. He was still in his clothing, which was, he sensed, very dirty. But his shoes were gone. He pulled himself up to look at his right leg. The old woman put her hands on it.

Pat yelled. His back arched. He yelled again. The dog

barked. But her hands worked. The pain sickened him. He began to black out. He fainted.

The old woman poked and pried at the bones with her small strong fingers. Then she went off to another part of the house and came back with more rags. She began to bind up the leg, winding and pulling, crooning to herself.

"Johnny's come home. And I'll take care. Nobody knows and nobody shall know. No more. No more."

Out in the front room of the old bungalow the dog let go and flopped suddenly, and put his black nose on his paws.

After the rain stopped, Vee Adams listened to the dripping and the trickling and the soft shifting of the water, all around the house and yard. She sat at the dining room table, with her books spread out under the center light, just as she usually did on a week-night. As usual, half the time she sat dreaming.

Her father had not come home for dinner. He had not yet come home at all. Vee was hanging a dream or two upon his unexplained absence, resigned to having the dream shattered and Everett come in, wet, and anxious lest Celia have been troubled. As if Celia cared.

Her young stepmother was lying on the couch in the den, nibbling and sipping and watching TV, just as usual. She had claimed not to be feeling well, all day long, but Vee wasn't worried about her health. Celia had these spells of total lethargy and, on the whole, they were somewhat easier to bear than her spells of restlessness. Vee had done, as usual, what she conceived to be her duty, bringing Celia what food she asked for, being polite.

When her father had married two years ago, Vee had

been enchanted. Celia was so darling, so beautiful, so mysterious and sad. Vee had tried to imitate her, speak as Celia spoke, wear her hair as Celia wore hers. But when Celia's health had improved and she was no longer quite so limp about everything, Celia had simply lost interest. She had never been mean or cross, particularly. She had just begun not to see, not to hear, not to notice a teen-aged girl in the house. And of course, since the day Everett Adams had first seen Celia Wahl, *he* had lost interest altogether. Vee had sensed that from the beginning.

So she had done her best to guide herself by clinging to what she could remember of her own mother, Lillian. The only thing she had kept from the first six months of Celia was the new version of her name. Celia had hooted at "Violet" and dismissed "Vi" as just too, too old-fashioned. So "Vee" it was. But in all else, Vee tried to be what her own mother had been and had wanted her to be—a little lady.

She chose and wore dainty dresses, in tiny prints and pastel colors and made with tight bodices and full skirts. She wore the daintiest little flat slippers she could find. Not for Vee the tight wool skirts, the big sloppy sweaters, the sneakers or the saddle shoes that were the current campus uniform. Or the sheaths and spike heels and the glitter.

She was a bit of an odd-body on the campus. A professor's daughter had a count against her in the first place. A town girl, living at home—that made another. Vee had never been a joiner. She hadn't been asked much.

She went her own way, a way that was so lonely and miserable that it had to have the compensation of these dreams. A Prince would come, who would see at once that there was only one Real Princess. Celia would die and her father would take a Sabbatical, and he would take Vee abroad, where she would be an American Princess, mysterious and sad. Mrs. O'Shea would die, and Mr. O'Shea would be devastated; only one heart would have the gentle understanding that would bring him back to life. Vee would die . . . or almost die . . . and everyone would be very very sorry.

To Vee, death was romantic.

When her mother had died, her father had romanticized it and canonized a meek and colorless woman. He and his little girl would go on, courageously, sustained by her memory. That was before he had gone to Los Angeles one weekend and there, somehow, somewhere, encountered Celia Wahl.

Celia had been a waif, or she had seemed to be. It had been almost a year before her brother had turned up. Vee tried never to think about Cecil Wahl at all. He was too much for her and she could fit him into no dream whatsoever.

But where was Dad? After all! Now that the storm was long over, and it was getting late, a shaft of true anxiety pierced through.

Vee began to close up her books and notebooks and pile them neatly, ready for tomorrow. (Lillian had been very neat.) Then she went through the long living room of this conventional and Lillianish house, which was not modern but not really old, either, and very little touched or changed by Celia.

Celia was in a long blue garment, a kind of housecoat that zipped all the way up the front. She was propped up upon many pillows, smoking, watching the screen through half-closed green eyes. Her feet were hidden under a bright afghan. Her ash-colored hair was loose and unkempt. Her face was not made up, nor was it even clean. Celia was still beautiful. The air was close in here, full of smoke and perfume and the mysterious fragrance of Celia's flesh.

On the coffee table were some dirty plates, a cup half full of cold tea, a telephone, a big ashtray heaped to overflowing, some magazines, a dish of hard candy, and three bottles of nail polish.

Vee knew better than to speak while the program was on. She stepped quietly and picked up the dirty dishes, dumped the cigarette butts upon one of the plates, carried these to the kitchen, washed the dishes. She went back to stand in the door of the den and wait for a commercial. When it came on, she said, "I'm going to bed now. Did you want anything more?"

"I guess not," said Celia. She didn't turn her head. Her feet twitched under the afghan.

"Are you going to wait up for Dad?"

"Hm?" Celia's eyes squinted against smoke. "Oh, I don't know. Where is he?" Her fair brow puckered. It was as if the question had only now occurred to her.

"I saw him leaving school," said Vee. "I told you." Celia said nothing. "He forgot I was supposed to ride home with him." Celia's shoulder made a tiny shrug. "Mr. O'Shea left right after him," said Vee with a small bursting out of her need to be noticed. (The rest was in a dream; she wouldn't tell the rest.) "He might know."

"Pray who," said Celia coldly, "is Mr. O'Shea?"

"He's on the faculty. You've met him." Celia just looked at her. "I know you have," said Vee stubbornly. "He's the one in the office right across from Dad's."

Celia's eyes simply left Vee's face and turned back to the TV screen.

Vee turned her back and went away. She crossed the living room and went upstairs. She had locked no doors, turned off no lights. Sometimes she got so tired of being the one to think of everything. She hurried to her bed because there the dreams came easily. She would phone Mr. O'Shea who would come, saying "Poor brave . . ." No. Mrs. O'Shea wouldn't let him. But he'd be sorry. Her father would die: Celia would be sorry. Then Vee could say what she could not now, loyally, say to anybody.

Downstairs, in a few minutes, Celia reached for the phone and dialed a long number. She was smiling faintly.

"Yes?"

"C?"

The man's voice said, aside, "It's only my sister, honey." Then it said, "Yeah, C? I wish you wouldn't call here."

"Something's funny."

"What?"

"He hasn't come home tonight."

"Well?"

"I don't know."

"What do you think?" said her brother sharply. "He's baring his little soul?"

"Probably he's drowning his little troubles. Maybe he got rolled." She giggled.

Her brother made a sound of exasperation. "Anybody been there?" She didn't answer. "They'd have come by now," he said. "Does he . . . write things down, C? Is there anything around?"

"How would I know?"

"Look."

"I wouldn't know where to look," she said with a sultry stubbornness. "Or what you've touched in this house, either," she added and heard his breath catch.

"Nobody's been there?" he said in a moment. "Maybe I'd better come by, C?"

"Do," she said on a soft pure note.

The wire carried nothing for a second—but something, just the same. "I'll see you, C," he sighed, and hung up. She hung up and hugged herself.

Upstairs in her room, which was as neat and dainty and beruffled as Lillian had thought a little girl's room ought to be, Vee lay on her bed and dreamed with her eyes open. After a while, she began to wish her father would come home. There were some dreams that might be too exciting and too terrible, if they ever were to come true.

An hour later, Vee sighed, got up and went softly downstairs, where the lights still burned, the TV still ran, pouring forth some late late show. Vee, feeling prim and in Lillian's skin, went into the den and turned off the TV. She took up the afghan and pulled it higher to cover the sleeping form of her stepmother. No use trying to rouse her and get her properly to bed. Celia didn't care. She had no idea of propriety, no order, no routine, nor any sense of time or duty. Just was. Was Celia. Everett Adams might be enchanted still. His daughter was not enchanted anymore.

Vee put out the light in the den, left one light on in

the living room, in case her father came, locked the front door, went back to her own place. She crept under the covers, thinking with honest pain that she was probably the loneliest person in the whole world. Quickly, she wove the healing dream. If anything terrible *had* happened, then she would just go away somewhere. Alone. Mysterious and sad. Somebody would notice. . . .

On the dot of midnight, Anabel O'Shea uncramped her legs from their huddled position, went to the phone, and called the police.

"I would like to report that my husband hasn't come home," she said, "and I am afraid something's happened to him."

"May I have your name, ma'am?"

"Anabel O'Shea. My husband is Elihu O'Shea, but everybody calls him—"

"Address?"

"3407 Pine."

"Does he drive a car, ma'am?"

"Yes. A Rambler."

"Can you give me the model, color, and license number?"

Anabel gave him this information precisely, in the same order, visualizing a paper before him, some kind of form to fill out.

"What was his destination?"

"His what?"

"Destination? Where was he going?"

"Why, he should have been coming home," she said, feeling a ripple of exasperation. She could understand the four-syllable word. It had just seemed an odd word to choose.

"Where was his point of departure, ma'am?"

"The University. The Science Building. He is an in-structor—"

"When and where was he last seen?"

"Listen, I don't know. The point is, I haven't seen him. I'm afraid that he's had an accident or he's hurt—"

"He had identification on him, ma'am?"

"Well, I suppose so. Of course he did."

"We'll check the jail, ma'am."

"The jail!"

"Yes, ma'am."

"But why?"

"If he has been booked for some traffic violation, such as drunk-driving, he might not be able to get in touch."

"He was not drunk-driving," she cried. "He is *missing*. He isn't where he should be, where he was expected." (All right, she could condescend, too.)

"You'll have to come down to the station, ma'am, and make out a report on that."

"Report?"

"Yes, ma'am. Missing Person report."

"Come *down* there?"

"Yes, ma'am."

"But it's midnight. I have a small child. I have no car. I can't—"

"In the morning, ma'am. That is, if he hasn't gotten in touch by then." It was obvious that the voice assumed her problem would vanish with the dawn.

"But there was that terrible storm," she cried. "And he would have called me."

"We'll check the jail, ma'am," the voice repeated patiently. "And you come down in the morning."

"Thank you," she said dubiously. They hung up. Then she was suddenly very very angry.

Jail! Anabel had been astonished by the word. Now she was angry at the very thought. Angry with that policeman. Angry with Pat, too. How could he do this to her?

Anabel yanked herself around. All right. *He couldn't.* And she was getting angry so as not to be afraid.

She got out the phone book that had the yellow pages and began to call every hospital in town. Had they a patient, brought in this evening, named O'Shea? No? Then, had they an unidentified man about thirty? No? Finally there was no number left to call and she perceived that, in the middle of the night, with Sue asleep, with no friend living close by, or even, in fact, a friend in this town that was, in any sense, close enough, there was nothing more that Anabel could do except see to her own state.

Anabel King had been a normal, happy, all-American girl. Raised in comfort (if not luxury), sent to good schools, always popular, always successful (at least in middle terms). Been wooed and won, had a lovely wedding, a wonderful honeymoon, a darling baby girl, this cute house, and many projects for a good happy future . . . with, all along the way, the usual "problems" to give life spice. . . .

She left the light in the bleak emptiness of the living room, went into their bedroom, crept into their cool bed, resolved to go to sleep. After all, Sue would be up and shining very early, and Sue must be taken care of. That was something that Anabel, all-American young mother, could and must do.

But with her hands tight on the edge of her pillow and her nose buried, Anabel King O'Shea, female person, prayed as hard as she knew how to pray. Let him be all right. Let it be something silly that I haven't thought of. Just let him be all right and let him come home.

Then she lay, groping for what could now sustain her, and thought, Up to now, nothing—not even Daddy's death —nothing really bad has ever happened to me.

Tuesday

TUESDAY had a gray dawn. The storm had washed the land. In the hard light, everything was startlingly clear. Yet there was no sunshine.

Anabel lifted little Sue out of the taxi, paid the man and, taking her child by her soft little hand, led her into the police station. Even in her anxious weariness, it struck her that this was a strange thing to be doing, early on a Tuesday morning.

When she stated her business, she was sent to a room and to a desk within the room, where a very young man in an ordinary suit gave her the paper and the pen. In her own writing, Anabel put down all she had said on the phone last night, and a description of Pat besides. Age: 31. Height: six feet. Weight: 180. Hair: brown. Eyes: blue. Scars: none. How meaningless! she thought. How perfectly undistinguished! Shouldn't I put down "Very intelligent. But lighthearted. A gay and loving man"?

She kept her head down and asked, "What else?"

"Has he ever been in any trouble? Any misdemeanors? Traffic violations? Drunk-driving?"

She said stiffly, her tears staunched, "I have never known him to be drunk." (Were the police *obsessed* with drunk-driving?)

"Doesn't drink at all?"

"Of course he drinks," she said a little impatiently. "Socially, moderately. But he does not 'get drunk' and he is a good and conscientious driver."

"He is not wanted by the police, ma'am?"

She said stonily, "Why should he be wanted? He is not a criminal." Anabel's heart was beginning to pound. "Why do you ask me these things?" she demanded. Little Sue, sensing the gravity of this expedition, was being very good, quiet as a mouse, standing in the shelter of her mother's left arm. Anabel thought, She is only four. She won't remember, will she, these insulting questions about her Daddy?

"Has he any known enemies?"

"Any what?"

"Is there any reason to suppose," said the young man, with just a trace of weary patience, "that he has met with foul play?"

She said, staccato, "Yes. There is. He didn't come home."

The young man went on, blandly, "Was he in an emotional state, Mrs. O'Shea? For instance, had there been some dissension between you?"

"Nothing important," said Anabel in a moment, trying to remember that he must have been trained, he must only be doing what he was supposed to do. His face did not change but his mind closed. She seemed to see it close. She said sharply, "Nothing like that."

"Is he in debt?" the young man continued impassively.

She stared at him. She couldn't even answer.

"Is he happy with his job? Or is he restless, would you say?"

Anabel said, forcefully, "What are you talking about? Do you think he might have run away? Leaving me to just wonder?"

The young man said coolly, "I'm sorry, ma'am. Could there be, do you think, some other woman?"

Anabel leaned toward him. He had very smooth, clean-looking young skin. He was a good-looking lad, a type she knew—the young buck, arrogant of his youth and strength. To such, she, aged twenty-eight, was already an old *bag*.

She said, speaking very distinctly, "If you will listen to me, I'll tell you what kind of man you must look for. A highly intelligent, highly educated, highly respected, successful, happily married, devoted . . ." She had to stop before her voice broke.

The young man had waited for her to stop. Now he smiled at her and she could have hit him for the pity in his smile.

"But I suppose," she said, "you have your statistics, don't you?"

"Yes, ma'am," he said. He picked up the paper that she had signed. It was a gesture of dismissal.

"What will you do now?" asked Anabel.

"We'll hold this for twenty-four hours."

"Hold it!"

"After that, we'll probably put out an APB on his car."

"A what?"

"An all-points-bulletin, ma'am."

"But for twenty-four hours, did you say? You'll do *nothing*?"

"That's right, ma'am."

"Don't you understand?" she cried. "Or don't you believe me?"

"Yes, ma'am." His young face was cold.

"What is your name?"

"Carlson, ma'am."

"Who is your superior?"

"That's Captain Murch, ma'am."

"Where is *he*?" If he called her "ma'am" once more, Anabel might scream.

The young man said smoothly, "Unless we have some reason to believe that there may have been foul play, it is the policy of the department—"

"I told you the reasons." Anabel stood up.

"Captain Murch isn't in the building, ma'am," he said, lightly, as he rose. He was watching her.

She hung on to her control. She could read in his eyes his expectation of hysterics, for the handling of which no doubt he had also been trained. It was the child who suddenly began to cry.

Anabel gathered her daughter up into her arms. "May I phone for a cab, please?"

"Yes, ma'am. Certainly." Oh, he was just as glad she wasn't going to have hysterics. He didn't want to have to bother with them.

Anabel thought to herself an iron thought: They won't help me. I'll have to find Pat by myself.

Once at home, Anabel put Sue down among her dolls and phoned her mother in San Diego. "So will you come, Mom? And will you drive? Because I'll need a car."

Susan King, in San Diego, said, "Of course I'll come,

dear. I can be on the way in about twenty minutes. I should get there by noon."

"Oh thanks, Mom." Anabel was proud that neither of them had wept or wailed. Her spine was stiff. Her heart was bold. She called the Provost of the University.

Miles Drinkwater, the Provost, had a rich tenor voice well-practiced in the art of rolling out phrases of sympathy and reassurance. But when she told him that she had been to the police, Anabel sensed his dismay.

"I am so sorry you felt you had to do that," he said. "I am sure he is all right, Mrs. O'Shea, and you will hear from him soon."

"I can't imagine," said Anabel severely, "what makes you so sure. I, on the contrary, am quite sure that there must be something that keeps him from coming home, or calling me, and I want to know what it is. The police will do nothing to help me for twenty-four more hours. Will *you* help me?"

"Certainly," he said. "Certainly—whatever I can do, Mrs. O'Shea. Although I think we must keep our heads."

Anabel's head felt in fine shape. "Then will you please ask around, there at the school, whether anyone has any idea where he might be?"

"Why, I . . . er . . ."

"You won't?" Anabel was sharp.

"My dear lady," said the Provost, "I simply hope that you are needlessly alarmed. Of course, I want to do all I can . . ."

Anabel said, "I am glad you realize that I am alarmed. Thank you."

She hung up, not violently. Then she put her fingers violently into her hair and held tight to her own skull. But she pulled the phone book to her in a moment, opened it to the yellow pages, and began to call all the hospitals once more.

Miles Drinkwater got up from his desk, smoothing his jacket with both hands. He was most reluctant to "ask around" and thus spread the news that O'Shea hadn't been home all night. Surely it was a private and personal matter between O'Shea and his wife, and the Provost did not like to contemplate scandalous rumors. Mrs. O'Shea would be wiser, he thought, not to risk them. When the young man turned up, no doubt sheepishly, *he* certainly would not appreciate the broadcasting of this escapade among his colleagues and his students.

But, since the matter should be handled with as much discretion as possible, he had better handle it himself. Mrs. O'Shea was in no mood to be discreet. Unfortunately. So, reluctantly, and reflecting upon what multitudes of problems he had seen require no solution at all, given enough time and inattention—nevertheless, he left the Administration Building and walked across campus to the Science Building, nodding benignly in progress.

Joanne Knowles, the girl on the divisional switchboard, was quick to understand the Provost's desire for discretion. She told him what she had already told Anabel, that Mr. O'Shea had left at his usual time last evening and, as far as she knew, in no kind of state, except perhaps a bit of a hurry. She quite agreed that there should be no gossip and the Provost rewarded her with one of his most benign smiles.

He went down the corridor to O'Shea's office, and finding the door wide open, clicked his tongue. But the tiny cubicle was perfectly neat and perfectly empty. It had nothing to say.

He crossed the hall to tap on the closed door opposite, but Adams did not answer. His door was locked, as was proper. The Provost surmised, and even seemed to remember, that Adams had an early laboratory.

The students were now streaming through the building, giving the usual impression of total confusion, although each individual was purposefully going somewhere and would get there. The Provost stood in his little island of unbuffeted space, given as due his rank and authority, and looked benign. One of them had the temerity to approach him. "Mr. Drinkwater?"

"Yes, Mr. Parsons." The Provost was proud that he had the knack of putting names to faces.

"If you are looking for Professor Adams, sir, he wasn't in the lab."

"Thank you very much." Oh, the Provost knew Mike Parsons for what he was. It was the Provost's business to know these things. This boy was eaten with curiosity about the Provost's presence here, but he would learn nothing. By speaking four words, from Olympia, the Provost rendered him helpless.

Then he himself went back to Joanne Knowles to discover the number of the classroom where O'Shea ought to be at ten o'clock. He realized that he had harbored a somewhat irrational hope that O'Shea, whatever had kept him from his home, would have been here, attending to his duties. He lingered now, still half expecting O'Shea to come hurrying along, late but apologetic, and publicly correct enough.

O'Shea did not come. Finally the Provost sighed and turned his steps to the classroom.

It was full of rhythmic noise. The students were doing a countdown. Required by rule to give an instructor ten minutes' grace, they were now, all together, counting down the last minute.

The Provost's entrance stopped the noise abruptly. He went to the front of the room and faced them, summoning up all his guile. "I am sure that you will all be very sorry to hear," he twinkled at them, "that Mr. O'Shea will not be taking this class this morning."

Some of them accepted his invitation to cheer softly.

"However, I would like to ask those of you who had occasion to speak to Mr. O'Shea and perhaps, also, any of you who saw Mr. O'Shea, let us say, late in the afternoon, yesterday, to remain a few minutes. The rest of you may go."

He nodded benignly.

The class rose and began to shuffle out. Had he not come, he knew, they would have gone whooping forth. As it was, they went slowly, with backward looks.

How he hated them! The Provost clamped down on the familiar surge of this emotion. Damned smart-alecky kids. Oh so shrewd, so bright-eyed, so quick to use their potent energies for troublemaking. But so unteachable, most of them. So full of their own conceit. Hypocrites. Apple-polishers. Always trying to fool their elders, get good grades for no honest work done, work some angle . . . Smart alecks!

He gazed out of the window, wearing his own mask of benign calm. When the shuffling had died away, he saw that only one student had remained. She was the Adams girl, who stood before him, demure, eyes cast down, feet tight together.

Vee Adams had known, the moment she came downstairs on Tuesday morning, who was expected today. Celia was up, washed, dressed, and she had neatened the house. She had even cut some iris from the neglected garden and was in the kitchen arranging them. She was gay: she said she felt better.

Well, then, Cecil Wahl was coming. Vee knew these signs. Oh, the two of them, with their pale heads and their green eyes! Her father never saw the two of them as Vee had seen them.

Vee poured herself coffee and took her bun, which she ate standing, as usual. She could see, out the window, the open empty one-car garage. She said, "Dad didn't come home all night? But where is he?"

"I really don't know," said her stepmother, inclining her fair head. "With a friend, I imagine. I wouldn't say anything about it, Vee."

"About what?"

"Why, about your father having his little night on the tiles?" said Celia, looking mischievous, her green eyes crinkling up.

Vee choked on the bun, put it down, and left the house.

When the Provost made his request, Vee saw her plain duty, as Lillian would have seen it. Vee had promised Celia nothing, really. She owed the Provost some obedience. Now the distinction of being the only one who had anything to tell him pleased her.

The Provost was looking at the open classroom door and

canceling his impulse to shut it. He knew better than that. He said to her benignly, "Miss Adams. Miss Violet Adams."

Vee lifted her eyes and said, "I happened to see Mr. O'Shea driving away, sir, last night."

"Ah, did you?" He was giving her his full attention.

"I happened to be waiting for my father in the faculty parking lot."

"I see. And Mr. O'Shea left in his car, did he, as usual?"

"He left in his car."

The Provost was a fox. He took in the evasive precision of her answer. He understood a little about this young person. So he said, with a confidential air, "I know that *you* will not spread this rather distressing bit of news, Miss Adams. I am concerned, you see, because Mrs. O'Shea tells me that he was not at home last night, at all. So she begs me to question anyone who may have any notion . . . You do understand?"

"Yes, sir." But Vee's heart had leaped and she was afraid.

"What is it, my dear?" the Provost purred kindly.

"Nothing."

It was a female "nothing." The Provost ignored it. "I hate to see you look so troubled," he purred on.

"Well, it's my f-father."

"Ah?"

"He drove away so fast he didn't even wait for me. And Mr. O'Shea jumped into his car and drove away too." This man was so kind and discreet. Surely she could tell him this much.

"And it seemed strange to you?" said the Provost in a tone that was careful to muse and explore.

"Because my father wasn't home last night either," the girl blurted.

"Well, then," said the Provost, smoothing his vest. But it wasn't well. It was astonishing. He didn't know what to make of it. "You don't know where either of them may have gone?"

"No, sir. But it wasn't the usual way. They both turned around the Science Building toward the gym. I . . . I had to take the bus home."

"Is your mother worried, my dear?" cooed the Provost, wondering to himself when yet another wife would phone him.

"No," said Vee. Her face turned pink. "*She* isn't worried at all. But *I* am."

"I don't wonder." He touched her shoulder, exuding sympathy and understanding. (The Provost had remembered Celia Adams.) "Of course you are worried, but there'll be some explanation, you'll see." (Privately, he imagined there would be a story invented, for the child.) "Thank you very much for staying to tell me this. But I . . . er . . . wouldn't . . . I think it might be a disservice to your father to . . . er . . . mention this to anyone else. That is, until we know the truth. Don't you agree?"

"Yes, sir, I do agree," said Vee with pathetic gratitude.

"Now then, if anything more occurs to you . . ."

He saw her swallow.

"Is there anything?"

"No, sir."

"Or, if you are too much worried, please be sure to come to me. You will, won't you?"

"I will. Thank you, Mr. Drinkwater."

Vee moved, making a little ducking motion that suggested an old-fashioned curtsy. Then she went out of the classroom with her head high, her back straight, her feet taking small dainty ladylike steps.

Odd girl, the Provost thought. For one thing, she will be quiet.

Then he saw a thin figure pass swiftly by the open door and glance in, with a sharp nose pointed. Parsons. Oh, so smart, oh, so sharp, oh, so bright-eyed—some of them were, when it was none of their business. When it could make trouble.

The Provost left the classroom, walked to the east corridor, and went along it to a window at the end which overlooked the faculty parking lot.

He knew that behind him, at the drinking fountain, there were students and he knew that one of them was Parsons, that he was on the scent somehow and making capital of it with his contemporaries. He knew they lingered there to watch him, to wonder, to buzz, to glean what they could. Oh the little foxes! How he hated the whole pack of them!

Life would get them, of course, he thought with savage pleasure. They'd find out. They, too, would become middle-aged. Their bright promise would also fade. They, too, would be stuck, and only if they were very very lucky, stuck in a place where there might be some honor and the salve of some daily respect given. But neither would they— any of them—set the world on fire.

The parking lot had some empty slots. It told him nothing. He walked back, passing the group of innocent children at the drinking fountain and nodding, benignly. He knew how "innocent" they were not. How eagerly they could condemn, without proof or knowledge, an elder to the punishment of their sly and nasty laughter.

On the way out of the building, a student named Rossi stepped aside politely. To him, the Provost did not nod. How stupid, the Provost thought, it is to steal!

There had been daylight, now, for some hours; nobody had come.

The old woman had fed him a breakfast consisting of a porridgelike substance and a cup of bitter tea. She had done for him the necessary, helped him to his animal functions in a stolid, matter-of-fact, and unembarrassed fashion, for which he tried to be grateful. But she made him very uneasy.

His head was better this morning, but the flesh above his ankle was swelling against the binding rags painfully, and his hand, he knew, was not what it ought to be. But the head was no longer splitting and his mind worked. Pat considered his situation.

When he had wakened in the dark, he had heard the animal, somewhere beyond a wall, mutter recognition of the fact that he had wakened. He had tried to sit up; the dog had growled. Then he had heard the creak of furniture and imagined the old woman's body turning, in that other room. His head had been fuzzy and his notions of place and space confused, his notion of time quite unreliable.

Considering the situation, then, he had thought that Everett Adams would send help soon. So it was not worth the effort to try to put his weight on his right leg, to hobble, hop or crawl out of this refuge, disturbing the old woman from her rest. Nor could he do it without disturbing her, since he had nothing on but his undershorts and a bandage. He had no idea where his trousers were, and no notion how to make a light in the dark and alien room—much less make his own way, in the night, over unfamiliar terrain, painfully, toward a telephone.

Considering all this, he had let himself drift and, eventually, he had slept.

But soon after first light, he had begun to conclude that Everett Adams was not going to send help. It did not seem possible that help had already come, to search that eucalyptus grove and, finding nothing, had gone away without at least asking questions at the door of this house. Would Pat have heard them? Yes, he would. The dog would have heard them and raised a racket. No, help had not come, not all night nor at dawn, either.

Remembering the look in Everett's eye and the stone raised in his hand, Pat knew, now, that he had run into something more serious than a theft. Adams had been beside himself—which was a very fine old phrase, and meant exactly what it said. Now, either he was in collapse somewhere, suffering the pangs of a terrible guilt, gone out of his head entirely—or, he was without conscience in the matter and might have even thought it desirable for Pat to have died where he had fallen, injured, exposed to that storm. Ridiculous! Pat wasn't going to *die*, of course. But he really ought to have some medical attention.

Very well; dismissing Everett, there was still Pat's car. Surely, standing there abandoned at the end of the road, it would be noticed by somebody. Anabel would be starting up some kind of search for him by now, in which a description of his car would have to figure. Then, questions would be asked at this door and he could call out. . . .

So he had thought, in the dawn. But now he knew that his car was not there. Or so the old woman had told him.

Mrs. Pryde. Ought he to believe her? Had she even understood the question? Could she observe with any accuracy? Or did she answer out of her delusions and her desire?

Four times he had patiently told her his name, his address, his station in life, and four times he had begged her to send for a doctor, send to a phone, notify people. Four times she had ignored his words, quite as if she hadn't heard them at all.

She was not deaf physically, but he suspected that she was psychologically deaf to some words. Any words that would take her son away from her.

He knew, now, that she and the dog had found him lying in the grove unconscious, that she had fetched a blanket and rolled him upon it, and then she and the dog had dragged him to this house. Dragged him up the stoop, into the house, into this room, where she had somehow managed to heave him up and on this bed.

Before the rain.

Remembering the deluge, he realized that no trace of this progress would remain for a search party to find, which was unfortunate. But he would be found, of course.

Still, adding everything up, Pat knew he could put no hope in Everett Adams who possibly—probably, in fact—had gone off in Pat's car. And he feared that it would be some time before the searchers that Anabel—oh poor Anabel!—would no doubt put to work, could possibly discover this road, this far, dead end of it, and knock on this door. Therefore, Pat had better do something about his situation himself.

Convince the old madwoman that he was not her son Johnny Pryde? Or just get out of here and find sane people?

But now, at midmorning, he had to concede that it wasn't

going to be easy to get out of here. His leg was a mess. He was not the strong and agile person he needed to be.

This room had one window at the back, one at the side, both old-fashioned sash windows, both hung with ragged lace curtains behind which cracked green shades were drawn to the sills. Even so, he could tell that there were screens on the windows although he did not think the screens were very strong. He could break out at a window, he guessed, but not without the dog knowing what he was up to. He certainly could not crawl, on hands and knees, fast enough to get away from the beast, especially when he had no notion in which direction, or for how far, he would need to crawl. There was no hope in speed. There was no hope to cover his tracks from the dog, either, by any kind of stealth.

But the dog was the woman's instrument. If she was not willing to let him go, then the dog would not let him go.

So he must convince her that she had no reason to keep him, that there was no relationship at all. Why should this be so difficult? He moved restlessly. He called out to her. "Mrs. Pryde?"

She came in, through the door to his left. There were two doors to this bedroom. The one directly before his eyes must lead into the front room, the living room, the "parlor" (he imagined), and in that room must be the front door that led to the weather. The door by which she now entered led, at least eventually, to the kitchen. There was a short hall with a door at its end, and a bathroom between.

Pat had hopped that far. Earlier, he had gotten out of bed, at least, and tried out his physical resources. He had rummaged in the bathroom, through the cabinet above the washbasin, and found nothing in it but a large can of talcum powder and a box of corn plasters. He had washed his hand in cold water. He had let the scab on his head alone. His teeth felt slimy. Never mind. His brain worked. His ears worked. He had heard the dog padding, his nails clicking upon linoleum, in the kitchen on the other side of that other door.

He now had a sense of the geography of this house. It was a square, or near enough. He lay in the back corner room. The kitchen lay on the other back corner. The living room must run across the front. For all he knew, there was a dining room, another bedroom, a room, on the far front corner, adjoining the kitchen.

What he could not place, could not remember, was this house in relation to any other house on Oleander Street. Or in relation to the inhabited world.

"Oh, Johnny." There she was. She was glad to come to his call. She was glad to hear him, to speak to him. Yet she had not been hanging over him. He had heard her muttering to the dog her litany, her "nevers" and her "no mores." But he could guess that she was unused to another voice, another human presence. And perfectly unfamiliar with any contradictions. Well, perhaps she would get used to him, and his words would begin to wear through. He did not know, now, how to get through to her. Was it any use, now, to say for a fifth time the words she had not yet recognized? Pat decided to try indirection.

"Tell me about Johnny Pryde."

He watched her accept this. He thought, She's in a divided state. One part insisted that he was Johnny Pryde. The other part knew very well that he was not, and this was the part that remained deaf, that would not hear. No, that was wrong. It heard. It knew. It would not let the other part know. The part of her that lived within a stubborn wall, not made of wood and plaster.

"A good boy," she said. "Good boy."

"Your only son?"

"Only son, only one."

The dog barked. She had been careful to close the kitchen door so that the dog was not able to come into this room with her. The dog was jealous, was he?

Pat had given some thought to what he could do, if and when the dog came bounding in upon him with hostile intent. Wind his arm in the bedclothes and thrust it into the dog's mouth? Yes. Possibly. If he were quick. But Pat wasn't at all sure that, having done this, he could then deal with so powerful a beast. Swaddle him in the bedclothes? Tie them around the dog, like a straitjacket? That would take a strength that Pat must summon up for his very life, if and when the time came.

Now he said to the old woman, "I can't hear you when the dog barks."

"Quiet, Rex. Quiet. Eh, Rex?"

The dog muttered, saying "I don't want to obey. I obey."

"Sit down," Pat said, "and tell me. Why didn't Johnny come home a long time ago?"

"He would come when he could," she said. "I knew." Her eyes slipped sideways as the gears slipped in her mind. "You're feeling better, Johnny? Eh, Johnny? You'll see." This was the happy half of her, and in that happiness lay his problem. The poor old soul must have been solitary here for years, and happiness she had not known.

"How long have you lived here by yourself?" he asked her.

"Straight here, I came, when they took you away. Straight here, to wait here. Because you'd know. Eh? Where to come. Where to come home, eh? I knew you would come." Saliva slipped over her lower lip.

"Where is Mr. Pryde?"

She shook her head. It was as if she couldn't remember such a person this morning.

"You have friends, though? Neighbors?"

She cackled. "They're scared of me," she announced proudly. "They don't bother me. No more. No fear."

"Mrs. Pryde, do you get any mail?"

"Never wrote. No mail," she said. "But I knew why, Johnny. I knew. All the time, I knew you'd come as soon as you could. And that was what you'd do."

"But you get some mail?"

"I don't bother. Mail don't bother me. Box is down the road," she said carelessly.

Pat remembered the lines of country mailboxes standing together at intersections, saving the mailman long journeys to solitary houses. No mailman would come to this door, then.

He said, "How do you live?"

"Eh?"

"How do you get food?"

"From the store," she answered. "No fear."

Pat narrowed his eyes. "That's the store at the other end of Oleander Street?"

"Johanneson." She was looking sleepy and contented. She had not sat down. She swayed, supported on two feet and the staff.

"You go to the store, then?"

"Ah, no—no more. No more."

"I don't see how you get your food then."

She cackled. "Why, the boy brings it. He comes on a day, then he don't come, then he comes, then he don't, then he comes and then he don't for two days, and then he comes again."

"Monday, Wednesday, Friday," Pat said aloud. (Today must be Tuesday, he reckoned.)

"What shall we have to eat, Johnny?" she said with sudden excitement. "What shall we have to eat, eh? What do you like? I know what you like. Meat. Meat, eh? I'll write down meat."

She turned. She moved quickly. She went off through the door and returned, almost immediately, with a small pad of paper and a stub of pencil. "I wrote down, already," she told him. "And Rex, he gets his meat—but you don't want that kind. Good meat, eh, Johnny? Eh?"

"That's right," he said slowly. "I see. The boy comes with an order and you give him the next order."

"Certainly, certainly," she said impatiently. "The boy gets my check out of the box, and I sign, and Mr. Johanneson, he takes care. He pays the bill for the water, and all. Nobody bothers me."

"Your check?"

"Pension. Pension," she said. "It's aplenty. No fear." She sat down on the one straight wooden chair.

"The boy comes the day after tomorrow?"

"Today," she said. "Today."

Tuesday, Thursday and Saturday, thought Pat, with a spark of excitement.

She was writing something on the paper now, laboriously. Pat watched her. Poor old thing, a hermit here. All her people dead no doubt, or somehow lost. And her only son in prison. He had figured out that much.

"Why did they put Johnny in prison?" he asked her, hoping to catch her unawares.

"For nothing," she said. "He didn't do what they said. It was them girls, them lying sneaking girls. Oh, they said he did terrible things. They said he come upon them in their cars and he beat their boys and he did terrible things to them girls. But they were just lying. He wouldn't do that. Johnny wouldn't do that. I knew he wouldn't do that. They didn't listen to me. But I knew they'd never keep him. Never. Never."

"Mrs. Pryde," said Pat, "could you please tell the grocery boy, when he comes, that I need a doctor? Or let me talk to him myself? Then I promise you I'll do all I can to find out about your Johnny."

But her ears had closed. "The boy don't bother me," she said. "Good meat, eh, Johnny? Beef, you like, and lamb too. But you never was a one for ham, eh, Johnny?"

He said for the fifth time, "Mrs. Pryde, my name is O'Shea. I am a teacher at the University. I live in town. I have a wife and a little girl."

"No more," she said. "No more. Nobody bothers me. No more. No cops. No doctors. Aplenty. Aplenty." She rocked from side to side, absorbed in bliss.

Pat said in a moment, "Is there plenty of bread?"

"Bread," she said. "That's right. Bread." She bore down with her pencil.

"I'll need some medicine," he said. "Write it down, will you?"

She didn't seem to hear.

"Ma?" he said.

Life flashed across her face. She'd hear him now.

"Doesn't the store have medicine?" he whined.

"Oh, yes," she said. "Oh, yes. Certainly. Certainly." All her wrinkles had curved up joyfully.

"Then write it down." Pat's wits were working. "There's one kind," he said plaintively, "would do me a lot of good."

"Rest is the best thing," she said happily.

"Comes in a bottle. You can put it on the order. I'll spell it for you, shall I?"

Her hands were still.

"Ma?"

"Eh, Johnny?"

"Put it down," he said, and began to spell, loudly, evenly. "P–O–S."

She did not move.

"I feel terrible." He rolled his head. "Don't you want me to feel better? Ma?"

"I know better than them doctors."

"That's right," he said. "No doctors. None of them. Write down the name of the medicine. P–O–S—"

Her pencil began to write.

"H–E—"

The pencil continued.

"A," said Pat. "Have you got it, Ma?"

"I got it," she said tenderly. "The boy can bring it, eh? And the good meat and all?"

"And fruit," he said. "Apples?"

The pencil wrote.

Pat thought, Oh, what nonsense! What do I think I am, the prisoner in the tower? Sending a cryptic note to the outside world, with my name hidden in it. Oh, come *on*. He sat up.

"Help me out of bed," he said loudly. "I want to go outdoors."

He let his legs over the edge of the bed. His right foot touched the floor and pain flared. He leaned on his hands and felt from his right hand a long stab go up his arm. He looked at that hand. The lacerations were pus and flame. He didn't like the look of it. "I want to go out in the sun," he said firmly.

She had her old lips pursed and they pushed in and out. He could almost see the gears shifting. "The sun don't shine today," said the part of her that knew he wanted to escape.

"I want some fresh air."

"The air's no good."

"Who's going to see me?" he challenged. "Kids maybe? You afraid?"

She put the pad in her pocket, and holding to the staff with both hands, she rose and swayed, looking down into his face.

"They don't come," she said. "Never. No more. I'm the old witch. That's what they think. They're good and scared of me, the kids are. And Rex, he knows how to keep them away. They don't bother me. Eh, Rex?" Her voice lifted.

Something in her tone communicated with the dog. The beast began to bark and snarl. His heavy body thudded upon the door.

Pat let himself slowly back upon the pillow.

"Down, Rex. Good dog," shrilled the old woman, with triumph in her voice.

She tucked the staff's end into her shoulder and came to lift Pat's legs. His right leg throbbed. But it was the hand that worried him. He said, "All right, but will you please boil some water and I mean *boil* it. And bring it and a clean rag and I mean *clean*."

He was feeling sickish. That door was so frail and he was in no shape to contend with the animal.

"My head aches," he said to her. "Keep Rex quiet, will you?"

"He's a good dog. Good dog."

"I'm sure."

"He minds me."

"Yes?"

"You mind me, too, Johnny. You mind your ma, and nobody is going to get you. Never. No more."

He said to her boldly, "Old lady, I am not your son and you know it."

"I'll take care," she crooned. "You'll see. You'll see. I don't mind. It don't bother me." She was leaning over, patting his left arm, and the mask of that crazy happiness was too close.

"Boil the water," he said feebly. "Ma?" He closed his eyes.

"Hot. Hot. Hot." She patted him. "You'll see. You'll see." He heard the rustle of her clothing.

Pat lay there when she had left the room and he saw, all right. The old woman was mad and he was her prisoner. Furthermore, unless he played up to her fancy, or whatever it was, this room and this bed were not even safe. She had a deadly weapon, which was the dog.

Pat took a little time to believe all this, including the flaws in the old woman's reasoning, and watching for flaws in his own. But there it was. And no living soul knew where *he* was, unless it was Everett Adams, who must be mad in some way of his own.

But then he thought of Anabel. Pat took no time to worry for Anabel's worry, for her confusion and her hurt and her fear. He had worried about that already. And she was well into that by now. He could not cancel out what she had already endured. And must still endure.

He tried to guess what Anabel would do. Go to the police. He felt sure of that. He relaxed a little. It might take a little more time, but it would not take forever. They would find him.

Furthermore, there was the grocery boy—sometime today.

Anabel's mother stopped her five-year-old Oldsmobile in the driveway at about a quarter to noon. She put her plump little feet to the ground and hauled a suitcase out of the tonneau in a businesslike manner. After embracing Anabel and searching her face, Mrs. King greeted little Sue with all grandmotherly comfort and good cheer. Anabel almost fell down with relief.

But not twenty minutes later, Mrs. King having taken house and child into her sure hands, Anabel was driving her mother's car over Pat's accustomed route to the University, feeling full of energy but a little confused by sudden freedom.

All morning, caged in and waiting, she had been scheming and plotting, pushing against the nothingness of no news at all. But, as the way wound through decent residential streets, she wondered how anyone was to know what dwelt in any one house, what innocence, what evil, and she saw the ordinary world, which only seemed to be buzzing along its ordinary way, to be perfectly opaque and mysterious.

She whipped the car into a familiar gas station and asked the man to fill it up.

"You get yourself some transportation, Mrs. O'Shea?"

"It's my mother's. Tell me, did you see Mr. O'Shea going by, last night, around dinnertime?"

"Can't say as I did."

"Would you have, I wonder?"

"Well, I was here 'til seven o'clock. See, I was waiting on the brother-in-law . . ." The man rambled on.

Anabel caught herself murmuring "I see" and looking wise and she thought, This is futile. This is only making talk. It's going through motions. The idea frightened her. She said flatly, "He never did come home."

"Oh-oh. Well, gee, I'm sorry, but I didn't see him." The male face became, in some subtle way, pro-male.

Anabel thanked him, paid him, and drove on. The ordinary world was not only mysterious—a good part of it might not even be on her side. But Anabel stiffened. Just the same, just the same, she must *do* something.

She crossed the highway and entered the campus through the main gate. She drove to the parking lot behind the Science Building, put the car in Pat's slot, went through the glass doors, up the metal stairs, along the east corridor. Joanne Knowles waved at her, looking startled. Anabel turned the corner and went directly to Pat's office. The door was open. The little space was quiet and empty. She went in and sat down behind the gray metal desk. Its surface was neat. She flipped the pages on the calendar. Saw one note, *Saturday, 8 PM Drinkwaters.* Oh yes, if he never came back, she would have that last silly squabble to remember forever. Anabel beat away the sentimentality. Come on now, she said to herself sternly. What you are going to do is this. You are going to look for Pat. *Look*, then.

But there was nothing here to see. No clues. The desk drawers were locked. Anabel had no key. Nothing on the bookshelves but the usual books. Nothing on the floor, on the other chair, on the clothes tree. Nothing on the clothes tree? Then he had his raincoat with him. And what difference did that make? A head came around the edge of the open door and startled her.

"Mrs. O'Shea?"

"Yes?"

"My name is Mike Parsons." A thin boy came sidling in. "Mr. O'Shea isn't here?"

"No," said Anabel.

"Well, uh, do you know where he is?"

"No, I don't. Do you?" she asked crisply.

"Well, uh, no, I don't, naturally. I just happened to see them take off, last night. First Evvy and then O . . . I mean, Mr. O'Shea. And it looked kinda funny to me at the time."

Anabel stared at him. "What time?"

The boy put his knuckles on the desk and leaned on straight arms. He fixed her with a stare. "Have you called the FBI?" he said, hoarsely.

Anabel shoved Pat's desk chair backward and put up her hand to beg for respite. "Just a minute. First, who is Evvy?"

"Oh, I'm sorry. That's Professor Everett Adams."

"Adams?" Anabel knew Everett Adams, having met him at faculty parties. She knew the daughter rather better.

The new wife she had met once or twice. Anabel didn't much like any of them.

"He's gone too," the boy said, with his air of portent. "Didn't you know? Look, they both took off. One right after the other. And fast. Evvy went tearing out of here. And then O . . . I mean, Mr. O'Shea . . . went tearing after, and they took off in their cars and nobody knows where they are. I mean it's kinda obvious." The boy stopped speaking and watched her.

"If there is anything that is obvious to you," said Anabel with dangerous calm, "will you please tell me what that is?"

"Two American scientists?" the boy said breathily.

"Well?"

"Well, shouldn't the FBI get on it?"

"On what?" said Anabel.

"Well, I mean . . . they took off. They're both gone" —the boy lifted one hand to snap his fingers—"like *that*. Something could have tipped them that this was the time. So if they're defecting to the East, probably the FBI could have stopped them from getting out of the country."

Hollows appeared in Anabel's cheeks. "Is this *your* idea?"

Joanne Knowles spoke from the doorway. "Anabel, excuse me, the Provost would like you to come to his office, please."

The boy took a step backward and muttered, "Who can help wondering?"

Anabel said, "If you *wonder*, then you think it is *possible* that my husband has run away out of this country because he is or wants to be a Communist. Or have I misunderstood you?"

"Listen, I only wondered." The boy shuffled his feet

doorward, but Joanne Knowles was a big girl and she was in the doorway. He looked back at Anabel. "That would be one thing you wouldn't know, would you?"

Anabel was on her feet.

The boy managed to duck around Joanne and get away. Anabel said to Joanne stormily, "You told the Provost I was here?"

"Well, I knew he'd want to see you. Listen, Anabel, he is only trying to stop a lot of talk and all that—"

"He's been doing just fine, hasn't he?" said Anabel furiously.

Anabel walked over to the Administration Building with such an air of angry purpose that people melted out of her path. She clacked into the building, raced up the stairs, and marched through Miles Drinkwater's secretary as if she had been made of smoke. But then Anabel said to herself: What are you *doing? You are looking for Pat.* Keep that in mind.

Miles Drinkwater was gallant with chair, cigarette, ashtray. Anabel endured these ceremonies, but as soon as he had put his rump solidly into his chair she said brightly, "Well? What have you done?"

"I am so glad you came," he said. "I'd been expecting you to telephone. Well, now, as far as I can determine, your husband left his office and the building at about five-thirty, which is his usual hour, and he drove away, toward the gymnasium."

"With Everett Adams?"

"Well . . . perhaps coincidentally." The Provost looked wary.

"But Everett Adams is also missing? Is that true?"

"Well yes. That is to say, he isn't here. But I cannot believe that there is any connection. I spoke to Mrs. Adams on the phone and she is not . . . er . . . too concerned."

"Does she know where he is?"

"Well, perhaps not . . . but she presumes that he was with a friend last night. If he hasn't taken his classes today, then perhaps something to do with this . . . er . . . friend has detained him."

"What kind of friend?" said Anabel stonily.

"I really can't say." But the Provost's tone was answer. "That, of course, is why she has not . . . er . . . spoken to the police. I daresay," the Provost purred on, "that the wisest course—"

"Mr. Drinkwater," said Anabel, "frankly, I don't give one hoot in hell where Everett Adams is." He blinked at her—this slim charming young woman who had always seemed to him to be the kind of wife a young teacher ought to have. "I want to know where Pat O'Shea is," said his wife. "What else have you done?"

The Provost fingered his pince-nez.

"Have you called the faculty together?"

"Since he . . . er . . . left at his usual time—"

"Or called the students together? Or in any way, broadcast for information, all over this place?"

"I spoke to his ten-o'clock class," said the Provost stiffly, "and received the information I've given you, which seemed to me—"

"Mr. Drinkwater," said Anabel, "you, and only you, could question this entire school. Not even the police could do that. But you haven't!"

"I . . . er . . . am inclined to think," said the Provost, working at a modified twinkle as best he could, "that your husband might be rather disconcerted, upon his return, if too much of a fuss were to be raised."

"Oh?" said Anabel. "Then you think he, too, spent last night with a 'friend'?"

"No, no, my dear young woman! I simply say that his absence would seem to have nothing to do with the University or his work here. Most plausibly, it is something personal and therefore his personal privacy ought to be respected."

Anabel said, "The police won't act because they think Pat should have time to come privately out of some drunken stupor, or get privately out of some floosie's bed. You have done nothing, really, because you wish to give him the same respect?"

The Provost was not liking Anabel much at the moment.

"Well," she said hotly, "I don't think anything of the sort. Shall I tell you what seems most plausible to me? Will you remember, kindly, that I know this man, privately, rather better than the police? Or you? Or anyone else? The only thing plausible to me—and I hope to God it isn't true —is this. Pat may have given someone a ride and that someone just hit him on the head, and dumped him out, and stole the car. That is the only thing that explains to me why Pat hasn't called me. It's because he *cannot*. He is not able. He is hurt, somewhere. Or he is dead."

"Oh, my poor child," the Provost said. "Try to believe that he will turn up and explain all this, quite simply. You must not upset yourself—"

"Oh yes, I must," she cut in sharply. "Tell me how you know that Pat left, as you say he did."

"Why . . . er . . . Miss Knowles saw him leaving the

building. And Miss Adams, Miss Violet Adams, saw him leave in his car."

"Vee Adams?"

"You know her?"

"Oh, yes. She's been at the house."

Anabel began to chew her lip. She had been hoping to find some clue that had to do with the school. But if there was none, then there was none.

The Provost said, "I really cannot believe that there's anything to worry too much about. Isn't it the wisest thing . . ."

But Anabel was not after the kind of "wisdom" that merely soothes. She said icily, "When and if Pat turns up, as you expect, he is going to be rather more than disconcerted to discover that he and Everett Adams are supposed to have defected to the Communists."

"What?" The Provost snatched for his glasses.

"That is what your student body is wondering. Didn't you know? Two American scientists. Both missing. To them, it is obvious."

"It's ridiculous!" cried the Provost. "Who told you that?"

"A boy named Parsons."

"Ah, that one." The Provost was furious. "Well, this sort of thing must be stopped, immediately." The Provost glared about him. He snatched his phone. "Get me Captain Murch at Police Headquarters." He nodded, sightlessly, at Anabel. "I know the Chief of Detectives, or at least *he* certainly knows who *I* am. Now, we'll see. . . . Hello . . . no, no, Captain Murch himself. This is Miles Drinkwater speaking and the matter is urgent."

Anabel sat mouse-still.

"Murch? You have a Missing Persons Report on one of our people, Elihu O'Shea, which you are holding. . . . Yes. . . . Now I am going to beg of you," the Provost let his voice go sarcastic on the phrase, "that you go about locating this man, and quickly. I'll tell you why. A Professor Everett Adams is also missing—more or less, that is—and we are being riddled by a rumor which must be stopped, and stopped once and for all, by an open exposition of the truth here, before the school and my faculty is damaged by talk of *this* kind. . . . Eh? . . . Oh, defected to the East, which is ridiculous! . . . No, no, impossible! Science teachers, certainly, but of no importance. . . . Now, you know very well, sir, how easy it is to start such a rumor and how difficult it is to stop one. So I must insist . . ." The Provost went on very forcefully but Anabel had stopped listening, two sentences ago.

He hung up finally and beamed upon her. "Captain Murch is assigning men to the case at once," he said, "and an all-points bulletin will go out on his car. They'll find him."

Anabel stood up. "Mr. Drinkwater."

He scrambled to his feet. "Don't thank me."

"I hadn't intended to thank you," she said, bluntly. "I'll tell you this. If it turns out that Pat is very badly hurt or if he is dead—and that, had the police begun their search at nine-thirty this morning when I first called you, he would not be in such a desperate state—then I won't forgive you and I won't let you off anything."

"Mrs. O'Shea!"

"If you knew this captain and could have phoned him hours ago but did not—and if *therefore* anything happens to Pat—"

"But please—"

"—who is of no importance—" said Anabel with glittering eyes.

"Mrs. O'Shea! I meant, to the enemy. Please, you are emotionally upset. Naturally. But let me call the infirmary—"

"It is infirm," said Anabel, "to care about what happens to my husband? In whom I believe?"

"No, no, of course not. I only wished to spare him—"

"That much respect?"

"I cannot talk to you while you are so emotional," cooed the Provost, retreating to Olympia. "Won't you go home now? And rest? The police—"

"No. I am going to look for Pat."

"My dear Mrs. O'Shea!"

"I have at least one advantage," she said. "I know some places *not* to look." She swept out.

The Provost polished his glasses. Young. Idealistic. Full of faith. But life would sour her, too. Probably it would. Then he snatched for his phone and demanded the presence of Mike Parsons here, at once. The Provost was going to clobber somebody.

He had been touched. Yes, he had. He was not pleased with himself. He was having a glimpse—very upsetting. A classical idea. Death was better than dishonor? What? In this year of Our Lord?

Anabel knew where not to look, but not where. Kidnapped? Amnesia? She had tried but she hadn't been able to take these alternatives seriously. Dead in a ditch, then? But which ditch? Anabel was crying, but she held her head high and clattered, by blind luck, in quick and accurate rhythm down the stairs.

The information counter could not locate Vee Adams.

The library had not seen her; she was not there.

Anabel walked the wide campus paths, wild with energy. But she mustn't waste it in busy-work. Knots of students swerved to let her by. She stopped none of them to inquire. I should wear a placard, a sandwich board, she thought, reading, *I am Anabel O'Shea, looking for my husband, who is missing. Help me, if you can.* For how could she tell which student could or would, and how could she ask them all?

She could ask one. If she could only find her. Anabel raced into the Science Building and demanded of Joanne Knowles the phone book. Everett Adams' home address burned into her mind. Then, a thought struck her. "Joanne, did either Pat or Everett Adams get a phone call, late yesterday?"

"Oh, no, I'm sure not. Anabel, I'm so sorry . . ."

But Anabel turned away. It wasn't that she had believed what that boy had suggested. But he had given her a vivid picture of two men moving suddenly. Why? Not because of a phone call, anyhow.

As she hurried down the stairs toward the parking lot, she caromed into a sturdy boy who steadied her.

"Sorry," said Anabel.

"That's O.K." The boy, whose name was Dick Green, had to get going to his part-time job at a gas station. He never had time to hang around. His days were full.

He wasn't quite sure who Anabel was; he looked after her a brief moment as she hurried away.

Anabel started the car, remembered something, turned to her left out of the lot. Toward the gym, the Provost had said. That wasn't the shortest way. The campus drive wound gracefully to a fork where she might turn toward the dormitories. But that made no sense. Anabel went on to the South West Gate.

Nothing to see. Just the ordinary street. The usual traffic. The people of the world, coming and going. She blew out her breath, made a left turn across traffic, proceeded to a spot just outside the Main Gate after all, and so back into town.

The house was an undistinguished two-story tan stucco. Anabel had never been here before. She poked the bell.

A man opened the door and Anabel took a backward step, trying to remember where she had seen him. He was not as tall as Pat, yet he was tall. His hair was a very pale color, his face smooth and of a design familiar to her. His eyes were green, and inquiring, and, as if irrepressibly, they were also admiring.

"May I see Mrs. Adams, please?"

"I'm sorry," he said pleasantly, "but Mrs. Adams isn't feeling well at all. Could I . . ."

"Is Professor Adams at home?"

"He isn't here. I'm sorry."

"Is Vee at home, then?"

"No." Now the man smiled to apologize for all his negatives. He had fine teeth. "I am Mrs. Adams' brother. My name is Cecil Wahl."

"I am Anabel O'Shea."

"O'Shea?" He tilted his head.

"Will you please ask Mrs. Adams if she'll see me? I think she might, since both our husbands are missing."

"I see. I see." He threw the door wide, instantly. "Come in, Mrs. O'Shea," he said warmly. "Of course. I'll ask her."

Anabel stepped into the foyer, gratified by this response.

"Come in, and please, be comfortable," the man said in an anxious, and yet irrepressibly gay, manner. His green eyes were not missing any of Anabel's feminine charms as he led her to the living room.

The room was dull and even shabby. It seemed old. It had no clear line or dominant idea. It didn't seem the background for Celia Adams, whom Anabel had met at a few faculty gatherings, to which Celia had come, dressed in a high fashion unsuitable for these occasions. If Celia had a circle in this town, Anabel was not of it, nor did Anabel gossip in her own circle about Professor Adams having married so young a wife. If anything, Anabel supposed she felt a bit sorry for Celia, as a displaced person—but never sorry enough to have been much interested.

She saw that there was an open door at the far end of this room in which the man stood and spoke, very distinctly and quite loud enough for Anabel to hear.

"C? It's Mrs. O'Shea."

"Oh?" The woman's tone was tinted with indifference.

"Do you think that you could talk a little? She says *her* husband is missing, too."

"Oh?" The female voice went higher and was less feeble. "Well, then . . ."

"Of course," he said. He turned and smiled. As Anabel walked toward him it crossed her mind that this exchange, so very open, so very loud and clear, was in some way unnatural.

But she concentrated on the sight of Celia, struggling to lift her head. She was lying on a couch, her pale hair spread, her face smooth, her eyes green. "Don't move," said Anabel quickly. "I'm sorry you're not feeling well."

"It's this misery in my tummy," Celia said, sounding childish.

Her brother was putting a straight chair behind Anabel, who thanked him and sat down. He moved to the couch and perched, seeming to make himself light, on the narrow edge beside the afghan that covered his sister's lower body. He said to Anabel's wondering gaze, "Twins. That's right."

"I'm sorry if I was staring. . . ."

"We're used to it. Aren't we, C?"

His sister didn't answer. She seemed to be studying Anabel through long pale lashes.

"I thought I'd better come," said Anabel rallying to her purpose, "because it is so strange. Pat—that's my husband —left the Science Building last night about five-thirty and so did Professor Adams and . . . You *haven't* heard from him, have you?"

"No," said Celia. "No, we haven't." She seemed faintly hostile, now.

"C called me in the middle of the night," said Cecil Wahl. "So I took the bus over from L.A. this morning. Now she has this 'misery.' I wish she'd let me call a doctor."

"It'll go away," said Celia.

"You were worried?" said Anabel. "But you haven't called the police?"

"Have you?" said Cecil, pleasantly.

"Oh, yes," said Anabel. "And I suppose they'll be talking to you, now, because . . ." She told them what the Provost had done. Celia's only reaction was to roll her head restlessly. Anabel thought she must be in pain.

The brother, however, was looking keen. "The Provost called here this morning, didn't he, C? He didn't seem quite so . . . excited about it, then."

"He wasn't," said Anabel dryly, "until he found out the rumor that's going." She told him what the rumor was.

"Oh, Lord," said Cecil Wahl.

Anabel couldn't help it. She had been talking to him. The woman on the couch didn't seem to have his instinct to chat, to exchange, to make ease between strangers. He was now twisting his handsome mouth to a shape, part mirth, part scorn. "That's pretty damn silly, if you ask me," he said.

"It sure is." Anabel found herself smiling back, almost comfortably. "But where," she brought herself to her problem, "where *are* they?"

The man responded to her change of mood at once. "That's the question. Well, we've been pretty sure that Everett's off on some . . . oh, toot or other. Do you think they are together?"

"I can't imagine why they would be," said Anabel. "Can you? That's what I came to ask you."

Celia said, "I can't even remember anybody 'O'Shea.' O'Shea," she repeated, rather distastefully.

Cecil said, "Well, *I* don't know what to think. Unless Ev is where we thought and your husband is somewhere else . . . maybe where you've thought."

Anabel told him what she had been thinking, about a vicious hitchhiker.

"I guess," he said sympathetically, "you can't help wondering these days." He looked a trifle smug—or was it mocking?

"But," continued Anabel, "if there are *two* men in *two* cars, then that doesn't seem possible. Does it?"

"You are right," he answered promptly. "That would be different. But we don't know it wasn't coincidence. This is a cockeyed world, you realize."

"That's what the Provost . . ." Anabel began. Then she was struck by an idea. "But surely the Provost told you that Pat O'Shea was missing too?"

"I don't know," said Cecil quickly. He glanced at his sister.

Her green eyes were wide and round. He bent to her. "Don't be scared, C," he said softly. "Probably nobody hit Ev on the head. He's probably quite all right and he'll be coming along soon." His soothing sentences were overdone.

"He might be dead," his sister said, monotonously.

"No, no." He looked around at Anabel; his eye was warning, challenging and also flattering her.

Anabel said, "I don't mean to frighten you."

Celia said, "Well, I can't help anything, now."

"Of course not," said her brother quickly. "Of course you can't. You lie still. Lie still, C. Don't even think about it. Excuse us?"

Anabel rose and he went with her into the living room. He was rubbing his short fair hair. "Oh, boy," he said, looking sideways with irrepressible mischief, as if to say, "Look at me, in such a fix. I am not the type, really." "I think I am going to have to call the doctor. And I suppose I had better call the police, too. I certainly don't think she is in any shape to let *them* in on her."

"You may have to go there," said Anabel helpfully, from her own experience. "You may have to make out a Missing Persons report. That's what I had to do. They'll ask you all kinds of questions."

He was listening, with a cocked eyebrow.

"Is he wanted by the police?" Anabel went on. "That sort of thing. And they'll want to know everything about his car. Then they look for the car, you see. Some marvelous cure-all, called an APB."

He grimaced. His eyes, irrepressibly merry, appreciated her bitterness. "How can I go there, when C's the way she is? Well, I'll see." He didn't say so but Anabel knew she was being nudged to leave. She started toward the house door.

Still Anabel, however much she had been gratified by this man's quick responses or by his irrepressible admiration for herself, was not forgetting her real mission. Something else perplexed her. "But didn't Vee tell you that she was the one to see them leave in their cars?"

"Vee?"

"She saw them. So I understand."

"Vee's a funny little kid," he said thoughtfully. "I'll talk to her." He had an uncanny way of communicating without words.

Anabel said, quickly, "You are going to be busy." She went to the house door.

He reached around her with his left hand to open it. He said, "Listen, about cars . . ." Anabel almost, in the shelter of his body, looked up. "They look for cars, you know," said Cecil Wahl, "because they can spot a car. But a man, loose on his feet, has no license plate. Or make, model, or a too obvious year." He grinned.

"I see," said Anabel.

"I don't drive a car myself," he said. She was thinking that this was irrelevant when he added, "Darned if *I* could describe Ev's car. Could you?" The last was whimsy.

"If your sister can't, then probably Vee could," she reminded him.

"I suppose." He smiled.

"Well, thank you."

He was still smiling down. "On the other hand," he said gaily, "in this cockeyed world, your husband could be home, right now, pestering the police to find out where *you* are. Good luck, Mrs. Anabel."

Anabel sighed. She went down the walk to her mother's Oldsmobile, feeling chastened. She seemed to have been in contact with . . . what? Something experienced. Something not as painfully direct as she tended to be. Something that lived in a cockeyed world and did not permit it to surprise him. He didn't even take it seriously. She seemed to understand now why, the situation being what it was, Mrs. Adams had not called the police or raised a fuss. She seemed to understand . . . it seemed to have got into her mind in some underneath manner . . . that Vee Adams was no kind of objective reporter of facts. Perhaps the two men had not left, in any way at all, together. Anabel also seemed to understand that she herself would do best to rely on the police and their methods, because they were sophisticated. She had been naïve.

Beyond all this, as if in a spell, she drove home as fast as she could because Pat might be there.

Pat was not there. The police were.

Cecil Wahl closed the front door, crossed the length of

the living room, went into the den, sat down where he had been before. "Cops," he said. "Now we know. So, when they pick up our Ev, what is he going to say?" She hunched one shoulder. "I'd better know, C." His voice held warning. "And right now, before the kid gets home, or something pops."

"How do I know what he'll say, the old fool?" said Celia petulantly.

"I can be good and lost," said Cecil lightly, "in an hour or even less. On my feet, without a license plate. What I want to know— Is this trip necessary?"

She raised her head. "Let's go, C?" she said, eyes bright, lips ready to smile.

"You? With a tummy-ache?"

She let her neck muscles go limp again and watched him out of green eyes.

"Take ten minutes and run it all the way through," he invited. "You took the gadget from the lab at the college. Right?"

"Right," she said, mechanically.

"Told me to sell it and keep the change. Said it was Ev's contribution to my general welfare."

"I thought it was Ev's gadget," she said sullenly.

"Maybe so. You can be pretty dumb at times. And you can't tell me many lies, C."

"He said he couldn't lend you any more money. Then he was showing that silly thing off, C. He said it cost five hundred dollars. Well?"

"Oh, you did it for me." Her brother cocked an eyebrow. "But after a while, you told him what you'd done? And how was that again?"

"Oh, he was carrying on. I don't know. He's such a fool, C."

"That's when he phoned me. And I played stupid, said I'd thought it was his, and his contribution. Said I'd cashed it in. Hadn't the money to buy it back. Then what?"

"You made a mistake, C," she murmured.

"All right. Believe it or not, I didn't have the money. Now, I need to know exactly what Ev said *then*."

"Said the police could recover stolen property. Said the only thing to do was tell the whole story and ask for mercy. Blubbered all over the place. Said I'd taken what I'd thought was his, and they'd have to believe me if he believed me. Said you'd sold stolen property but you'd get off, if you hadn't known that, and if they believed you."

"Ah, we're getting to it. *Now*, exactly what did you tell him?"

"Well—the police, C? I just told him that if the police got into the act at all, they'd pick me up for murder."

"Pick *you* up?"

"I told him they had my fingerprints from that whisky glass."

"*Your* fingerprints?"

"Because he wouldn't give a damn whether they picked you up or not," she said, rather heatedly. "So that's why I lied. To shut him up, C."

"I wish you'd had more imagination," said her brother. "Why did you lie on the edge of the truth? You know damned well that my prints were on that glass."

"I know," she said, wide-eyed.

He stood up. "Not me," he said. "Not on account of the fat man conking out, five years ago, from one Mickey, which was practically an accident. I've paid," he said. "I've never put my thumbprint on a driver's license in the State of California."

"You don't have to anymore."

"Go on," said Cecil. "What did Ev say to *this* revelation?"

Celia giggled. Then she turned her head, cheek to pillow. "He said it was practically an accident. He said I was only a child five years ago. He said I'd never had a chance. He knows a little bit about Mom. I'd had no moral training." She was mimicking, now. "But I was a human soul and he would save me." She had a perfect mouth, but it went crooked. "Just about what I thought he'd say."

Her brother's mouth twisted, too. "Mom, being dead, isn't going to get picked up for rolling the fat man. Right, C? Nor am *I*."

"You left me," she said wildly. "And I was so sick. And he took me out to the desert. And he's saved me, already. And I can't stand it much longer. . . ."

"Done is done," her brother said calmly. "Now, Ev sent the money. I got the damn thing back. He had it yesterday. What happened, yesterday?"

"Nothing."

Her brother took two steps. Away.

"He was going to sneak it back into the lab, somehow," said Celia. "That's all I know."

"Did it get back there? I wonder."

"You wouldn't let me ask the Provost." She rolled her head.

Cecil ran his tongue around his fine set of teeth. "I've got something going for me in L.A. that I don't want to run out on if I don't have to. But this ice is pretty thin, C."

"Oh, probably he's dead," she burst, "he must be dead, or he'd be whining around here."

Cecil said nothing.

"If he is dead," she said watching him, "I get half."

"Half of what?"

"This house." She could cock her eyebrow, too. "Some bonds."

"Be right nice," drawled Cecil, in a moment, "if our Ev was dead. Who can be sure? What about this O'Shea? What could *he* know?"

"Nothing. Ran out on his wife. I wouldn't blame him." Her eyes were greener.

Cecil's mouth quirked. "A square, Mrs. Anabel. Pure and simple." He looked thoughtful.

She looked up at him. "C?"

"Yeah, C?"

"Don't go." Sweat broke on her brow. "If this damned thing didn't hurt me . . ."

He looked down at her, the green of his eyes cool and cruel. Her eyes met his with the same look, a cool acceptance of the existence of cruelty in a cruel world. "As it is," she said, "if you do go, why should I care where? It might as well be jail."

In a moment he smiled at her, as if he appreciated and even admired her use of threat. He touched her cheek. "Everything might work out," he said lightly. "It depends on where the old fool is."

Her head wagged over and imprisoned his fingers between cheek and cushion.

"I'll call the doctor," he said. "You be sick. And silent."

"All right, C." She was smiling, not looking at him.

"When Vee shows up, be sick. And silent. Or—a little bit worried? That's not a bad idea."

"All right." Her eyes closed.

"She doesn't know anything, does she?"

Celia's lids were tight.

"C?"

"No," said his sister, writhing. "There it goes." Her eyes popped open. "I'm scared, C. Something's wrong with me."

"Keep your mind strictly on your health," her brother said amiably. "That's the idea." He stretched lazily, without haste, for the telephone.

Pat was dozing when the dog gave tongue. He lifted up on an elbow. The old woman spoke; the dog broke rhythm. Pat thought he heard a horn blow. The dog began again.

The old woman began to shout and when the animal at last subsided, Pat could hear her saying, "Guard, Rex. Eh, Rex? Stay, Rex. Guard."

Was she going to the front door? Would she open it? Had someone come? He listened hard, waiting for the exact moment when he could most effectively shout his name and the news of his plight to any sane ear. He heard the door close, sharply. What? Had someone shown his face there, in perfect silence?

Pat got out of the bed. His leg was impossible; he crawled. His head throbbed, his hand hurt, he paid no attention. When his ear was near the bedroom door, he heard the dog growl low, on the other side. Pat could feel the vibration. He did not dare try to open that door.

But what must he do, then? Crawl, now, to the window?

Burst through, get out, *now?* Was anybody there? Had he heard an auto horn?

He became aware of a loss of pressure in the house, something was not in it that had been in it. The old woman had gone out! That was it. So Pat yelled. On the instant his throat opened, the dog barked. The dog barked and Pat yelled and the thin wood quivered between.

Stan Simmons looked nervously down from his panel truck at the old woman who stood there, at the broken gate, with her box of groceries in her arms. "He can't get out, can he?"

"He can't get out," she said. "No fear. He's a good boy." She looked merry and sly.

But Stan's spine was crawling and he seemed to hear, at twenty yards, the very thud of the beast's body on the walls. The dog was hysterical or something today. There was an almost human cry in the animal throat.

"Well, O.K., Mrs. Pryde," he said. "See you the day after tomorrow." Stan made the truck move and turned it, recklessly, in his panic to get away from here. "Dog's getting about as nutty as she is," Stan muttered to his dashboard. "And one of these days, it isn't going to be safe."

When the old woman had struggled up on the stoop and in at the door with her load, and had soothed the dog, and had come the roundabout way through the kitchen, Pat was back in the bed, staring at the wall.

She was puffing; she had the big carton in her arms still. "See," she said, putting it on the bed, "I told you. See here, Johnny?"

"Didn't the boy help you with that?" said Pat drearily.

"He don't get out of his truck even. Never. Never." She

cackled. "I told you he don't bother me. See here, Johnny? Pretty? Eh?"

He didn't want to turn his head, which was swimming a little. His eyes felt hot and almost ready for childish tears. He felt that he had failed, hadn't been quick enough, brave enough, smart enough. His head rolled and he could see her, taking the packages of food—the few cans, bottles—one by one into her hands and caressing them. He thought she was pitiful as she feasted on these. The gay colors, the clever shapes, the handsome labels of commercial packaging. For how many years had such things been her only news, her only pleasure?

"They are pretty," Pat said gently.

He thought, If I could make friends with the dog—that would be a way.

Stan bumped along Oleander Street, stopping and starting. Mr. Johanneson kept his trade by his delivery service. After all, if people had to get out a car, they might as well go to some big supermarket.

Stan made one special stop at Jamie Montero's observation point.

The little cripple was the whole street's pet. His father had been inspired to build him this perch, which even had a canopy for summertime. Here Jamie was King. No other child was allowed to share his throne, but the children liked to play around it. So Jamie was in the weather and in the world, and by no means shut away. And Jamie knew everything that came or went on Oleander Street.

Stan tossed him today's tidbit, which was a banana. The boy leaned forward. "Did you look?"

"Sure thing," said Stan. "I was all the way to the witch's house and I looked real good, believe me. This killer wasn't there."

"But he didn't come back."

"You ought to forget it, you know that?"

"I didn't see him. The nice man, yes. I saw the Rambler. But not the blue Chevy."

"Listen, you missed him. That's all it is, Jamie."

"I didn't sleep all night, Stan."

"Aw, go on. You dozed off." The little boy was shaking his head. "Then he went by in the rainstorm."

"I don't think so," Jamie said. "Nobody went by in that rain. Tell Mr. Johanneson thanks for the banana, and you, too."

"You bet," Stan said, as he always did, and went on.

One of the policemen was the young man Anabel had met before. Carlson was his name. The other was an older man, a very ugly man, big nose, furrowed cheeks, blue chin, a totally bald head. His name was Maclaren.

Anabel's mother made the introductions; both men nodded and sat down when Anabel did. Mrs. King took up her chatty thread. No, as far as she knew—and wasn't this right, dear?—Pat had no relatives nearby. Just the one aunt in—New Hampshire, wasn't it? And a sister, in Maryland. It wasn't at all likely that he had gone to attend to some family crisis without letting anyone know.

Anabel asked whether they knew that a Professor Adams was also missing. But she knew that they must know. She could feel herself faking a question, making talk, wasting, not the time of those present, but Pat's time. Her purpose came flooding back, in all its purity, to stiffen her.

She told them, flatly and briefly, that she had just been to the Adams house, that Celia was ill, her brother there; they didn't seem to know anything. Vee Adams, the daughter, was the one to interview. When she had finished these statements the young man said he didn't suppose she believed there was anything *in* this idea that the two men had gone out of the country. His face was bland, his manner a shade too respectful.

Anabel, feeling as if she'd been slapped in the mouth, said it was ridiculous. Her mother began to amplify, chatting along, saying all the nice things she so often said about Pat and Anabel, and the two of them together.

The man named Maclaren kept quiet. Anabel forgot he was there. She watched this Carlson's young face for the infuriating skepticism that she had seen on it before.

When her mother ran down, Carlson said smoothly to Anabel, "About this—er—quarrel that you mentioned, Mrs. O'Shea. If he's trying to get even, where would you say . . ."

Anabel felt her top blowing, again. She had not mentioned a quarrel, but she had told him, just the same. And his mind had closed. She remembered. "I'll tell you the gist of this famous quarrel," she said. "He made a date, without consulting me, on a night when I wanted to go somewhere else. I didn't like it. Now, what kind of people do you think we are? Do you seriously imagine that Pat O'Shea could be so stupid, so childish, so small, and so mean, as to run away? Just vanish? Leave me and his baby—and his job, too, by the way—just because I didn't want to go to the Provost's party and I said so? I don't care if your statistics say that ninety-nine percent of the people are complete morons.

Pat is *not*. Nor am *I*. And I'd like to ask you what you are doing here anyway?"

Anabel's top had now blown completely.

"You won't find him here, you know," she went on. "That he *isn't* here is the whole point! Or do you think he is hiding in the broom closet, to punish Mama?"

"Not at all," said the young man and his cold control only made Anabel worse.

She said, "What you are doing is busy-work! If you don't know that, then I'll tell you. Nothing but busy-work! It isn't really doing *anything*. It's taking time. It's going through motions."

Her mother said gently, "Anabel . . ."

Anabel stood up. She couldn't sit there. "But I keep telling him that Pat's in some terrible trouble," she cried. "That he *must* be. Why don't they *do* something?"

"We have an APB out on the—"

"Oh, well, then of course," she cried bitterly, "everything is just ducky, isn't it?"

The young man was looking grim now but still had the control not to answer.

The older man said, "One more question, Mrs. O'Shea. Might help us."

His very voice startled her out of her fit of temper and despair. It was a deep, warm, beautiful voice. She looked at him.

"Please tell us about his health," said this Maclaren.

"His h-health?"

"Is his heart all right? Or is he a diabetic? Anything like that, at all?" The beautiful voice was like a poultice upon the raw pain of her frantic frustration.

"No," she said with a feeling of clamping her head back

to her shoulders with two fierce hands, "no, he had a check-up in the fall and he was fine. He hasn't had his spring check-up yet. He's only thirty-one."

"If there was anything like that, you see," said Maclaren, "it might give us some idea *where* to look. In a pretty big world."

"I know," said Anabel, ready to bawl.

"That's why we try to find his car," said Maclaren, in gentle music. "Because to find it would certainly tell us a lot more than we know now, wouldn't it? The police of four states are watching out for it, Mrs. O'Shea, while we talk here."

"Yes, I . . . Mr. . . . ." She couldn't remember his name. "I'm sorry but I am so scared."

"Surely," he said.

"I know a car is easier . . ."

"It's a material object," he said, "and a big one. Statistically, we can usually find a car."

Anabel stood up. She had been clinging to the sight of the kind brown eyes in the ugly face, and to the sound of that voice. "Will you promise me you'll tell me? The very first thing? Whatever you find?"

"I promise."

"If I *could* help you . . ." She choked.

"God knows you would." This man believed her.

"Yes. Please, excuse me." She went blindly to her bedroom and fell upon the bed, and began to cry as hard as a woman had ever cried.

Mrs. King, without apologizing for her daughter, led the men to the door. They did not apologize, either. They got into their dark-colored unmarked sedan.

Carlson said, "Well, they do say that the wife is the last to know."

"This one knows," Maclaren said.

Carlson did not look at him. "Where to?"

"Up to you."

"The Adams bunch?"

"Fine."

Carlson made the car move. In a moment, Maclaren said, "You're new."

"As new as they come." Carlson was chipper.

"While I'm as old as they go, just about. And Friday night, I go. I guess you heard."

"Yeah, sure. I appreciate," the young man was cool and polite, "you're letting me conduct the—"

"I suppose I've got to say something," Maclaren cut in.

"Benefit of your experience?" said the young man lightly. "Captain probably thought of that."

"He didn't think of a thing. Drinkwater was on his back, so he sent two."

"Listen, what you were going to have to say . . . go ahead. I can take it."

"Maybe that's what I was going to say. Take it. *Some* people know what they're talking about. Otherwise, why be a cop?"

"Well, I'll tell you. It's a living, Dad," said Carlson blithely.

While Anabel bawled her head off, her mother did not come into the room but went about the house, tending to the child, the kitchen, the daily chores.

After a while, Anabel could weep no more. She rolled over on her back and stared at the ceiling through the red ruin of her eyes. Fat lot of good I did, she thought with her blood cold. I was going to find him. What did I accomplish? Got the Provost mad at me. Screamed at the police.

What to think, what to think, besides the awful thought that a car does not decay like flesh or even bone? No more of that. She thought about the Provost, and Mrs. Adams, and the brother. Funny that the Provost hadn't told them about Pat being gone or about Anabel's having been to the police. Why wouldn't he? Oh, he was just cagey. Yet . . . why hadn't Vee told her stepmother anything, either? Or had she? And was that Cecil Wahl the cagey kind?

Now there came back to her the fleeting impression, the first impression, that loud clear open passage between brother and sister that seemed to be proclaiming, "Look, nothing up our sleeves." Why should they think she might think there was something up their sleeves . . . unless there was?

Oh, come now. Maybe that Cecil was one of those people who go sideways, just in case.

But Pat goes straight. If Pat does not go straight, then I am the idiot of the world—which I am not. Pat does go straight. I believe it. I know it, or I know nothing.

This was the basis of her life and the very foundation of her woe.

Her mother put her head in. "Are you hungry at all, Anabel?

"Some," said Anabel. "What time is it?"

"Early. Only about five-thirty."

"That's twenty-four hours," said Anabel. Then, she grinned up at her mother. "Not long."

"Wash your face," said her mother gently.

Anabel got up and washed her swollen face.

When Vee came into the house with her load of books, she found Cecil Wahl in the living room. For once, his mood was sober. No, her dad was not here. Very worrisome. He was worried about his sister, too. The doctor was with her now.

Almost at once, the doctor came out of the den and phoned for an ambulance, saying he would get in touch with a surgeon immediately. So all was crisis and confusion.

When the doctor had gone, Vee didn't know what to do. But this was her home; she had lived here before Celia. She must be gracious, as Lillian would have been. She went to the door of the den and looked in on the two of them, Celia seeming spent and limp, Cecil with his hand upon his sister's brow. "I'm so sorry, Celia," said Vee, in Lillian's cadences. "Is there anything that I can do?"

Celia scarcely stirred her languid eyelids but Cecil took his hand away and said, "You don't have any idea where your dad is, do you, Vee?"

"No."

"You saw him leaving the school yesterday?"

"Yes."

"And you saw this Mr. O'Shea leaving, too?"

"Yes." Vee hung on to the doorframe. Two pairs of eyes stared at her now. So shallow-bright. So deeply cold. She would never let *them* know one solitary real thing about her. Such as a dream.

"Well?" said Celia, irritably. "Didn't you say this O'Shea 'might know'? What did you mean?"

"Nothing. Just that he could have seen. I mean, which way Dad went. Dad came out," said Vee, desperately stupid, "and got into his car. He drove away. Then Mr. O'Shea came out and got into his car, and he drove away." She stopped.

Sometimes Vee got a funny feeling about these two. They had their own odd ways, such as calling each other by the same first initial. For a long time, Vee had thought they kept saying "See." And they had other ways. They could agree, without saying anything out loud. They were like one, sometimes, instead of two, and uncanny. Then sometimes they were like two—and that was worse.

They were one, just now.

"For pity's sakes," said Celia weakly. "Is that all?"

And Vee was dropped, just dropped. Now she stood, unseen, unregarded, as if she didn't live here, or didn't even live. She didn't know what to do, or where to go. She drifted to and fro in the living room. When the phone rang, she started nervously toward the phone in the foyer.

But she heard Celia saying "Yes?" Celia was like a cat sometimes. She could go from being limp to being completely energized. Celia said, with friendly calm, "For pity's sakes. How are you?"

Cecil Wahl could move like a cat too. He sprang from his post at the far end of the couch in there and came swiftly to Vee in the living room. He took her arm and turned her, saying in a low voice, "Don't worry her about your dad right now, that's a good kid? She's pretty much in pain. . . ."

Vee pulled away from his touch. "You asked me," she said, ready to cry from the injustice of it.

"Then, I'm sorry. The police are looking for your dad, you know."

"The police!"

In the den, Celia said "Really?" on a long-drawn note. It seemed odd, because Celia didn't have the kind of friends with whom you gossiped on the telephone.

Cecil was rubbing his fair head. His body seemed to be crowding Vee. "They're looking for O'Shea at least, and they know your dad is missing too. So there isn't anything better that we can do. I'm wondering if you . . . Vee, will you help?"

"How?"

But his eyes were a little blind. He wasn't really seeing her. "I wish I'd asked the doctor. Listen, do you have any idea what C ought to take to this hospital? I mean, could you possibly get some of her stuff together?"

Everett was tumbling pent-up anguish into Celia's ear. "I can't tell you why, darling. I don't remember, now. I only know O'Shea is dead and I left him there and it's riding me and I'm sorry . . ."

She said, gravely, "I'm sorry, too." (He could not tell that her green eyes had swiveled toward the open door to watch the two figures in the next room.)

"I know I have to give you up. I only wanted to save you. If I can still save you, then I don't care for anything else. What is it to eat, to sleep, without my love? So I'm going to give myself up, my darling. I have to do that. There is my child to think about. In prison I could gather myself . . . gather myself . . . try to make her understand. But darling, remember I am the thief. I'll say so. He caught me. So I . . . well, I went out of my mind . . . I must have . . . and so I killed him."

"Are you sure of that?" she said rather gingerly.

"Of what, darling? But they must have found him!"

"Where?" said Celia, as if she were asking him to repeat.

He began to have a sense that someone was listening at her end. "At the dump," he said. "Where I left him. The old dumping place. I ran. Oh, Celia, I thought I had to think. Well, I have thought. It rides me, Celia. I am not the man to cast it off. You were not guilty, but I am guilty. I knew better." Everett sobbed.

"Why don't I meet you then?" she said brightly.

"What?" He was astonished.

"I'll meet you. I'd like to."

"When?" he said, on a tremendous sigh.

"Tomorrow?" (She was craning her neck, watching through the door.) "Let me see. Maybe not tomorrow. But the day after? Is that all right?"

"Would you do that?" Everett said, in awe. "Oh, my darling! Oh, God knows I was out of my mind . . . I never meant . . ." At his end, Everett was thrilling to a crazy hope.

At her end, in the living room, Vee said, "The simplest thing is to ask her." She took a side step to get away from Cecil, to get around him.

"Don't trouble her."

"If she can talk on the telephone . . ." Vee moved toward the den. She thought he hadn't been seeing her, he hadn't heard a word she'd said, he scarcely knew what he had been saying himself . . . a lot of silly talk about toothpaste, hairbrush . . .

She could hear Celia saying, "And if I'm late, just wait for me?" *Those* green eyes were seeing her, Vee could tell.

At his end, Everett was seeing a strange and unexpected glory. "Ah, yes . . . Ah, do . . . The two of us. Somewhere on this earth, surely . . ."

"It's a date then," Celia said crisply. "Just tell me . . ."

Cecil had moved faster than Vee and now he slipped around her and snatched the phone. "Who is this? . . . Oh, *Mary!*" He swung away, turning his back as his fingers cut the connection. "Mary dear, C is out of her ever-lovin' mind. She can't make any dates. She's on her way to the hospital, right now. . . . Well, we don't know how serious . . . I guess, not *too*. . . . An appendectomy, which isn't so much these days, even if it is—well, you know, a little quick. . . . Right, I'll tell her. . . . Certainly."

He put the phone down and said to his sister severely, "Are you delirious or what?"

His sister lay with her eyes shut. "I can't go to the hospital," she said in a sullen monotone. "I don't want to go. I'm not going."

Cecil hushed her, glancing up at Vee, his eyelids signaling a weary patience with a balky baby. "You just pack what you think," he said softly. Now *these* green eyes were really seeing her, and searching her somehow. "You'll have better sense about it. And thanks very much, Vee." Somewhere in the neighborhood a siren sounded. "Better hurry."

Vee ran across the living room and up the stairs. She didn't like Cecil Wahl. She never had. It was funny that he should be the first to notice how, in this house, Vee was the long-suffering mother-housekeeper and her stepmother the irresponsible child.

Cecil said, "Quick."

Celia said, "He says he killed O'Shea."

"How? Never mind. Where?"

"He said at some dump. 'Old dumping place,' he said."

"Where is that?"

"I don't know."

"What else? Quickly." The siren was outside.

"Wants to give himself up. Said he'd tell them *he* stole the gadget."

"Oh-oh. Our Ev will never stand up to a police interrogation." Cecil drew away as if, in spirit, he had gone a hundred miles.

"I know," she said stonily. "That's why I said I'd meet him. He'll wait."

"O.K. *I'll* go."

The doorbell was ringing. Two pairs of green eyes met, cool and cruel. "Probably he won't get to say anything," Cecil murmured, "which is best all around. Right, C?"

"Why bother?" she said, green eyes sliding.

"Come on. Where is he?"

"You grabbed the phone," his sister said drearily, "I don't know where he is. He didn't have time to say."

Cecil put his lips into whistle position but made no sound.

She lifted her torso. "And he'll call back, C. Sooner or later." The doorbell insisted.

"That's all right. I'll be here, C. I'll get it."

"Watch her, C. Watch li'l ol' Vee."

"Don't worry." He ran to let in the men from the ambulance, not noticing that, by some hocus-pocus, he had been induced to commit himself to stay around.

When Vee came running down with Celia's overnight bag, Cecil was on the phone in the foyer calling a taxi. The front door was wide open. They were lifting the stretcher into the ambulance. Vee didn't know what to do with the bag.

Cecil held the phone lower and said to her, "Look, you

can go along and sign C in, and all that, can't you, Vee?"

"No, I can't," she wailed, everything being too much for her, "I can't *do* it. Nobody ever sees me or hears me . . ."

"Then we'll both go," he said soothingly. "You certainly mustn't be left here, all alone."

She looked up at him. He was smiling. His teeth showed, but she seemed to be seeing them in a skull.

When Carlson and Maclaren pulled to the curb, the stucco house had a blank and empty aspect. The neighbor's twelve-year-old boy, big-eyed with the delight of telling news, said there had been an ambulance—sirens and everything! Naw, nobody was there, now, in the Adams house.

In the hospital corridor, on the fourth floor, Vee shifted from one foot to the other. White-clad people had brushed her aside. Celia didn't care whether Vee was in the room, or out here, or anywhere. Cecil Wahl had not come up to this floor at all. He was in the Admitting Office, or the lobby. Vee didn't know what else to do, finally, but try to find him.

She took the elevator. The hospital frightened her. She didn't belong here. (But where, then?) She stepped out into the lobby and saw a face she knew.

"Violet Adams," the young man said. "Hi, Vi. Remember me?"

"Beau Carlson." She could tell right away that he didn't like that old nickname anymore, but she couldn't remember his real name. "I mean—Mr. Carlson?" She was confused. This was a hospital. Somebody of his must be ill.

"I'm in the Police Department now. This is Lieutenant James Maclaren. Violet Adams. She was a frosh . . .

wasn't it, Vi? . . . when I was a senior, back in high school."

Vee couldn't get it through her head that Beau Carlson was really stopping to speak to her. He'd been a big wheel, a football player—in fact, *the* football player. The older man, with the clown face, wanted to know how her mother was.

"My stepmother?" Vee wondered how they knew about Celia. "I guess they are going to operate, just about right away. I'm looking for my . . . Well, I guess he's my step-uncle. Mr. Wahl."

She looked around the lobby. Cecil wasn't in sight.

"He's not around," said Beau Carlson. (How did they know about Cecil, too?) "Tell us about your dad, Vi. And this Mr. O'Shea."

(What did he know? Did he know *everything?*) Vee sucked in her breath. "Oh, you are *looking* for my dad," she cried. "Somebody told me."

(These are the police, she told herself, and the police are looking for my father. She didn't know whether to be frightened or not.)

"But you haven't f-found him?" she stammered.

"Not yet," said Carlson, "but we'll find them. Both. Why don't you just tell us what *you* know?"

Vee became rather stiff. She told them how she had seen both men leave, the order of their leaving, the direction in which they had gone. The older one asked her whether her father had seen her waiting there.

"I guess he couldn't have."

"Was it an appointment? Did he expect you to be there, Miss Adams?"

"Well, sometimes I wait for him. Sometimes I go home

another way." She wasn't going to say that she took the bus. Let them think she got rides with boys. Beau Carlson really was terribly good-looking. He'd been in the Service, she remembered. Now he was back and some kind of policeman. He'd be *good*, too. He was one of the lucky ones.

He began to ask her about her father's car and Vee stumbled through the best description of it that she could give. Imagine Beau Carlson remembering who she was! Talking to her, easily, as if they were friends—of old. She thought, When the time comes, I could tell *him* the secret that I know. He's the police and it's about a crime. She was gathering up material for a dream.

"I guess we can't talk to your moth . . . I mean your stepmother, right now," he was saying.

"There wouldn't be much point," said Vee, more frankly than she had meant to speak. "*She* doesn't know where my dad is."

"They don't get along too well?" He was interested.

The secret was in her mouth. (Celia is a thief. She stole something.) But Vee put her teeth over her lower lip. "I can't talk about that, really," she said primly in a moment, as Lillian would have said.

Cecil's fingers on her bare arm made her jump. "Ah, there you are, Vee. Gentlemen? I believe you were asking for me? I'm Cecil Wahl. I see that you've met Miss Vee Adams."

Beau Carlson began to talk to Cecil. The spotlight swerved and refocused. Vee was in shadow. She had a sense that the two young men were getting along just fine. Overtones went between them, two young bucks exchanging amusement at the antics of an old buck, as if they could understand what Vee could not. As if she hadn't known, for a long time, that her father was possessed, and it wasn't so very funny. They shouldn't think they were so smart.

Then, the one named Maclaren said into her ear, "You've had a rough time." It was just as if he had pushed a button. Vee began to sob. She was furious at herself for this. She hated herself. Cecil's arm came around her shoulders. She hated him and twisted away. She hated Beau Carlson, who took a step backward as if he resigned himself to the nuisance of her tears and would wait. She hated that other man. She was *very* brave. Didn't she go her brave and lonely way—mysteriously sad, perhaps—but a Princess, not a cry-baby? Vee hid her face from them all. (Except that there was no such a Princess. Just in the old baby-stories read to her, long long ago, when everything was better. When all you had to do was be a "good girl" and you would be praised and petted.)

"Poor kid," said Cecil.

Well, *he* just didn't know! None of them knew. Maybe *she* was the key to this whole business. So let them think she was just a "poor kid." Then, someday . . . A dream, to lean on.

On the way back to Headquarters, Carlson said to Maclaren, "Any of that get us anywhere?"

"Not far. Better check on this Cecil Wahl."

"He wasn't even in town."

Maclaren was brooding. Finally, he said, "Call it experience."

"Call what experience?"

"The knack of smelling them."

"Smelling *what?*" Carlson was very much startled.

"No, no," said Maclaren, "I mean the outsiders. The ones

who'd just as lief knife their old mothers as anybody else. The bums."

In a moment, Carlson produced a rusty laugh. "Excuse me, but he smelled to me like a young fellow just trying to get along."

Maclaren sank a little lower in his seat.

Carlson drove in silence for a moment. Then he said, in a light cool manner, "You've got another knack, I notice. Sure do know how to make the girls cry."

Maclaren said nothing. Carlson bit his lip and then said, rather angrily, "What hit *her*?"

"You used to know her, did you?" Maclaren murmured.

"Listen, I knew who she was. This Violet—in those days, strictly a pig from pigsville."

"That so, Beau?" The powerful voice was frosty.

"You know my name," the young man said stiffly.

"You a young fellow just trying to get along, are you? Or do you want to be a cop?"

"I am a cop."

"Then stop with the pigeonholes."

"What do you mean?"

Maclaren just sighed.

"Uh huh," said the young man in a moment. "But you can smell them. You got a pigeonhole for the bums. Right?" His voice was in control.

"I used my own nose," Maclaren said. "How did you know this Violet Adams was a pig? Was the word around?"

The lad blew air through his pursed lips, making them flutter. Then he turned his head and smiled. "Listen, I didn't mean to get out of line, sir. I appreciate you've had a lot of . . . experience. I'll try and learn. Don't call me Beau. O.K.?"

"The young lady seems to prefer to be called Vee these days," said Maclaren wearily, looking out of his window. "Don't call me 'sir.'"

"No, sir," said Carlson.

In the cab, Cecil said, "Vee, I wonder if you've got a girl friend who'd let you stay overnight?"

"Oh?"

"It might not be circumspect— Hey, that's a good word! —for you and me to stay alone in the house. Not that anything . . . But you know what I mean."

Vee felt like screaming and jumping out of the cab. Certainly she knew what he meant.

"Somebody you could talk 'female' talk to, anyhow," he went on. "I've got things . . . Oh, phone calls. Want to be on hand, just in case. How about it?"

"I'm trying to think." All Vee could think was that she couldn't go home to her own home. And when he said "female" talk, he meant stupid chatter.

"What about the neighbor lady? What's her name?"

"Mrs. Newcomb? Not there." (No, she *wouldn't*.)

"I've got a lot on my mind," he said, moving restlessly. "Could we drop you now?"

"You can drop me," said Vee regally, "any time."

"Give the man the address, there's a good girl," said Cecil, who bounced up in spirits now that he was going to be rid of her.

But Vee thought, It's *my* father. It's *my* trouble.

She gave an address.

Anabel heard the cab, looked out, saw it stop, and she burst the front door open. Coming up her walk were Vee

Adams and Cecil Wahl. She called out "Yes?" She was scared.

The man's feet broke stride, but the girl hurried ahead of him. "Mrs. O'Shea, I came to ask you, please, may I stay here tonight? Celia's in the hospital, and Dad's not found yet, and I thought . . . You are all alone too. I could help you with little Susie and be somebody around?"

"I see," said Anabel quietly.

Cecil Wahl had come nearer now. "Mrs. Anabel, I give you my word, I had no idea . . ." He seemed upset.

"Will you come in, both of you? Have you talked to the police?"

"Oh yes, they caught up with us," he said. "Not that we had anything to say. Look, I've got a cab waiting . . . Come along, Vee," he said sternly. "This is not a good idea. The lady mustn't be bothered."

But Vee stood still in the half-dark; the house light fell on her bent head and her clasped hands. She seemed to sway and catch her balance. Anabel distinctly caught her aura of being lost and in great distress. Great need. She had never liked Vee Adams. "Wait," she said.

"Really," said Cecil, "I thought she was directing us to some girl friend. There is no reason why you should put her up."

"There's no reason why not," said Anabel gravely. "Go on in, Vee, please."

The man moved as if he would physically interfere, but he did not, and the girl walked, with her head still bowed, up the few steps, past Anabel, and in at the open door.

"I'm afraid she'll be trouble," Cecil said. "She's a strange kid. Don't do this. It isn't necessary."

"You are going back to the Adams house?"

"I've got to be there, in case there is news, or something I ought to do." He was very uneasy.

"Your cab is waiting. She'll be all right."

"Yes." He hunched his shoulders and let them fall. "Well," he said, irrepressibly gay, "call it a star in your crown, Mrs. Anabel. Good night, and good luck to us all." He made her a jaunty salute and loped toward the cab.

Anabel went slowly into the house. Vee and Mrs. King were staring at each other. "Mother, this is Vee Adams. Professor Adams' daughter."

"But I thought . . ." The girl began to twist her hands. "I thought you were *alone*," she cried, "I honestly did." She had been crying.

"I believe you," said Anabel. "You haven't any night things with you?" Vee shook her head. "That's no problem. But have you had dinner?"

"I don't need any."

"Oh my," said Mrs. King. "But there's plenty left over. You come with me now—Vee, is it? I don't know whether you like leftover stew but it wasn't bad . . ."

Mrs. King swept the girl away with her on the tide of kind and hospitable chatter.

Anabel stood still, chewing her lip. The phone began to ring.

It was so silent, so silent, in the night. Sometimes a plane went over and noise bored through the high air. Sometimes a coyote barked, distantly. Otherwise, silence. No voices, traffic, footsteps, music . . . only the night, breathing around the old bungalow.

No moon? Those shades drawn, how could he tell? What night was this, anyhow? Pat's attention span was not what it ought to be. He kept starting a train of thought and drifting away from it and then finding himself unable to remember what it had been. Now, now . . . He rolled his head.

What had he been thinking? No guts, eh, O'Shea? That's right. Pursue that. So it would hurt him to walk on a broken leg? So what? He had a broken leg, a wounded hand, and a half-broken head. But that leaves half of me, he thought and grimaced in the dark. Half or more, and don't they say that half a brain is better than no brain?

How come I lie here and let a crazy old woman keep me here?

He lifted his head. Ah-ha, the dog hadn't heard *that*. How could he make friends with the dog when he never saw the dog? Only heard him. If he had any poison, he could poison the dog. He had never thought of himself as the kind of man who would ever poison a dog. . . .

Back. Back. He had been trying to think . . . What about?

About getting out of here. Sure. That was the only thing there was to think about. "And I had better think fast," he muttered, "because I don't feel so good, and that is a fact."

He heard the dog's toenails scrape on something. Bare floor?

"Got your ears up, boy?" muttered Pat.

Well, he said to himself, I'll tell you what. I'll just get out of this smelly bed and I'll get me over to that back window, and I'll put up that shade and I'll see what's to be seen, and if there's any light out there—or maybe even if there isn't —I'll bust the screen, I'll heave myself out of here . . . and what happens then is what is going to happen.

This seemed very simple, very clear.

He sat up and his head swam. The dog growled.

"Wake her up, then," said Pat. "What can she do? I'm Johnny Pryde, her Pryde and joy. So why will she set the dog on her own darling Johnny? Who is Johnny Pryde, anyhow? Where is he now? Where are the snows of . . ."

He caught himself swaying on the edge of the bed, thinking about something else instead of the project at hand.

At foot. All right. Pat got out of the bed. The leg didn't hurt so much at that. Or else it hurt so much, his brain wouldn't believe it.

She never left any matches around, damn it. He could have lighted the lamp. In fact, he could have lighted the world. Throw the lamp out the window. Takes a lot less than that to start the State of California burning. Pretty soon, fire engines.

"Fried alive," Pat said, quite loudly. "Fried alive, in my own grease? I don't care for it."

He guessed he wouldn't try to light any matches. Anyhow, he didn't have any matches. He didn't have any trousers, either. For my manly modesty, must I rot in this room? There comes a time . . . comes a time . . . when first things have got to come first and that's right and a man has got to sort out his values . . . and you can take the collision course because maybe you were wrong and you don't collide there wasn't anything there where was I?

He was standing, in a rubbery sort of way. The dog was giving out short yelps now. He couldn't hear the old witch moving or speaking, yet.

He tottered to the back window and, with his left hand, grasped the shade at the bottom and tried the little teasing tugging that would release the spring and send it up. But the spring no longer functioned. The shade tore from the roller, a quarter of the way across, and sagged crookedly.

Now the dog was making a lot of noise.

Pat brushed the shade aside and got it behind him. It was dark out there, but not perfectly black. There was light arched above—some kind of skylight? But clumps of blackness, knots and lumps of blackness. Trees? He couldn't see the ground. Dirty glass? He put his left hand (his right hand wasn't much use to him, since he couldn't open the fingers nor could he close them, all the way) . . . left hand on the lower sash, groping for a handle. Got it. The sash moved upward.

The dog was throwing himself at the door. *Thump.*

Pat put his shoulder against the ancient rusted screen and, as it tore, he pitched forward. The screen cut at his cheek. Now, wait a minute. He'd better not go out of here head-first, because his head was in no condition to be landed on. His half-head.

Like a swift dawn, light came up behind him.

"Now listen," he said, staggering on bent knees, half turning, "I'm getting out. I mean, that's all there is to it. So don't argue."

She was in the doorway and the dog was at her side. She had one hand on the dog's collar. The dog was muttering low. In her other hand, she held a lamp. She was wearing a shapeless gray garment. It was her nightgown. He could see her gnarled bare feet. He could see, and for the first time, something of that outer room. A patterned rug. A bit of carved mahogany.

He said, "Well, maybe the front door would be more convenient." His bent right knee would not straighten. All his weight was on the good left one.

The old woman put the lamp down on the chest of drawers. The dog crouched.

"Now, listen," said Pat, reeling, "I'm sick, old lady. I am as sick as a dog! Hah!" He raised his left hand and began to shake his forefinger at her. Once begun, the motion would not stop. "You want me to die? That's what you want? Eh, Rex?" He mimicked her. "Eh, Rex?"

The dog's feet scrabbled for a better hold. But the old woman made the dog stay and she came silently to Pat. Her strong hands went under his armpits.

Pat yelled. It hurt. The dog began to bark furiously.

"Quiet, quiet, *quiet!*" shouted the old woman. Then she said gently, "Johnny, you ain't well enough to go any place."

"Yeah, well, I know *that*." Pat sagged.

"Tomorrow," she said. "Tomorrow."

"Yeah, well—all right. Tomorrow."

She was helping him toward the bed and he was going there. She lifted his shaking legs. She pulled up the blankets.

"I'm burning," he said, throwing them off violently.

"No, no. No, no. *They'll* never burn Johnny Pryde."

"Never?" he said feebly.

"Never. Never."

His mind was drifting. "My mother died . . ."

"No, no," she crooned. "No, no."

"Tomorrow? Eh, Rex?" (That dog doesn't like me, Pat thought. I never did anything to him. Did I?)

"Tomorrow," the old woman said. "You'll see."

In a little while she left him, picked up the lamp and, in silence, ordered the dog to precede her out of the room. She shut the door.

"A touch of the influenza," she muttered to the dog. "That's what it is. Tomorrow the medicine will come, eh, Rex?" She padded on the dirty carpet to her nest on the couch. "Sleep's the best thing," she said. "Quiet now, Rex. Quiet. Mind." She blew out the lamp. "And the good meat, too. *I* know what's good for him. You'll see. You'll see."

The old house was dark and silent. Outside, the night breathed.

She said in the dark, suddenly, "The day *after* tomorrow, I mean. That's right. That's right."

Wednesday

ANABEL woke from heavy sleep and sat up in her bed. It was morning. It was nine-thirty in the morning. "Oh, no!" she cried aloud. The sound produced her mother, who said, "You were so exhausted, dear. I've talked to the police."

"Nothing?"

"Nothing, yet. I'll fix your eggs."

Anabel squeezed her eyes shut and dropped back to her pillow. That made two nights. Two nights and one day. Here was another day. Wednesday. And he wasn't here. And she didn't know where he was.

She made herself think about all the phone calls last evening. Friends, Pat's colleagues, acquaintances, even students—full of concern. And curiosity. But Anabel had developed a technique of turning the questioning the other way. Not one of them had been able to tell her anything. At last, she had become panicky and begun to say, as rudely as was necessary, that her phone must be left open for important calls.

There had been no important call.

When, at last, the phone had subsided, Mrs. King had

decreed bed for them all. They had made up the living room couch for Vee. Mrs. King was in the guest-room-den. So Anabel had come, again, to the big cold double bed, alone. Too exhausted to weep, too numb to pray, she had slept. Too long.

Although no matter, if there was no news yet.

She lay wondering where to get any purchase on the mystery. What about Everett Adams? Had he anything to do with Pat's disappearance? Was there anything odd about his wife and her twin brother? Why had Anabel taken Vee in last night? Why had Vee come?

Anabel knew that the girl was in the throes of a student crush on an attractive young instructor. Vee had turned up at this house several times, asking for special help, and Pat had given it, in his amiable way, at the same time warning Anabel that she must not, under any circumstances, leave the room where he and Vee Adams were. So Anabel had finished the best part of a sweater during those sessions. She didn't much like the poor silly kid—an adolescent poseur.

She knew that she hadn't taken the girl in last night for sweet charity alone, being under no illusion that Anabel O'Shea was pushing for sainthood. Nor had she done it with some superstitious notion that to turn any distressed person from her door would rebound upon Pat, somehow. Anabel now judged that she had done it partly because Cecil Wahl had not wanted her to do it, and partly because Anabel had hoped she might find out something. And partly for charity, after all.

But Vee had been very prim, forlorn, polite. Yes (she said), she had seen the two men drive away, first the one and then the other. She had said no more, *asked* no more, which was peculiar.

It had been Mrs. King who, after some friendly prying into Vee's affairs, had called the hospital to inquire for Mrs. Adams and had been told that Mrs. Adams had come through the operation very well and was resting.

Anabel threw off her coverings and jumped out of bed. But her mother's very charity and kindly wish to make the poor girl more comfortable had stood between, last night, and had prevented any detailed inquisition by Anabel of this girl who was, although a pitiable human being, yet also a puzzling one.

Meek as milk, but with the crust to come here and beg lodging.

Anabel bathed and dressed quickly, and sallied forth. Vee was in the kitchen, wearing the same small-flowered pink print dress. Mrs. King was trying to let herself be "helped."

"Vee couldn't go to her classes today," said Mrs. King. "For one thing, she'll want to go to the hospital. For another, the poor child has no clothing. Anabel, I wonder if you can't drive her to her house and pick up her things? It would be all right, surely, if you were along."

Anabel said, "Mother, go deal with Sue, would you? I want to talk to Vee alone."

Mrs. King read her daughter's expression and left them without protest or comment.

"Sit down," said Anabel, putting herself before her breakfast. Vee sat down the other side of the table. "You came here," began Anabel, "first, because you thought I might be all alone?"

"I did. I really did, Mrs. O'Shea."

"I know," said Anabel, "and I know you have a crush on Pat, besides."

"I—like him very much. He is a wonderful teacher."

"This is not," said Anabel, "the day to be mealy-mouthed."

Vee swallowed and turned her eyes.

"All right," continued Anabel with good humor, "I can't say that I understand it, entirely, but here you are. So since you were *there*, in that parking lot, I wish you'd tell me whether you think that the two of them went off together."

"They drove off in their cars." The girl's voice was low and it evaded. She was nervous. She was pitiable.

But Anabel snapped, "Don't be literal. I heard you say that before and I believed you. What I want to know, now, is this. Did it seem to you that there was any connection between the two of them?"

"I don't know." Vee began to sniffle.

Anabel said, "I'm not going to stop asking questions if you cry. Not when my husband is missing."

"My dad is missing, too," Vee mumbled defensively.

"All right. We are both worried, both scared, and we'd both like to know what's happened. So please tell me. Did they go together, in any sense at all? What did you think at the time?" she prodded.

The girl was using her handkerchief. "Don't pay any attention to what I thought," she murmured.

"Why not?" said Anabel, flatly.

"Nobody does."

"That's too bad," said Anabel. "But you're not worth much attention, the way you are behaving."

The girl looked up, startled and hurt.

"I am only asking for your opinion. Why can't I get it?"

"Because . . . because I'm probably stupid."

"You had a 'stupid' opinion, then?" said Anabel, undaunted.

Vee said, "Yes, I did."

"Well?"

"I thought maybe my dad didn't like it that I had a 'crush.' That's what *you* call it . . ." The voice was muffled.

"Why do you say that? That he didn't like it."

"Because . . ."

"You won't get out of answering now," said Anabel, cheerfully but firmly. "Go on."

Vee looked hostile suddenly. "I thought they were fighting," she said, "if you want to know."

"Fighting? Pat and Everett Adams? All right. You must have had some reason to think so."

"I did," said Vee. "Dad came out of the Science Building, almost running, and Mr. O'Shea came out and shouted his name. But Dad just ran to his car and took off as fast as he could go, and the wrong way, too, and then Mr. O'Shea ran to his car and took off right after him, and he was *mad*."

Anabel straightened very high in her chair. "Mad? Angry, you mean? You thought they were 'fighting'? About what?"

"I don't know."

"But you thought," insisted Anabel. "You had a 'stupid' opinion. What was it?"

Vee put her arms on the table and her head down on her arms. "Maybe my dad said something to Mr. O'Shea—about us. And honestly, Mrs. O'Shea, I knew you always watched us, but we weren't doing anything wrong. If I'm in love with him, I still . . . I *know* . . . I didn't expect . . . Well, I just think Mr. O'Shea probably got mad at my dad . . ." Her voice droned, dreamily.

"Over you?"

Vee sobbed.

"I see. Well, let me put it this way," said Anabel. "You are an idiot."

Vee's face came up, pink and startled.

"And you'd better get this romantic little opera right smack out of your romantic little head," said Anabel, with fairly good humor. "You kids, with your crushes, can be quite a menace. Pat always does insist that I stick around. He knows some of you get some pretty whacky notions and he'd better always have an honest witness."

Vee sat up straight, very red. "I didn't realize . . ."

"I'll tell you another thing you do not realize. If your father was silly enough to query Pat on the subject, then Pat would have told him, very kindly, how careful he knows he has to be. Not to guard you from harm, but to guard against the harm that you could do by what you call being-in-love."

Anabel choked off her rising temper. "Now, in the name of something more *like* love," she said, "tell me the truth. Did Pat shout after your father? Or did you just imagine how thrilling it would have been if he had?"

"But he did," said Vee, furiously. " 'Adams,' he yelled. And he was very mad, I mean angry."

"And they were running, you say? Hurrying?"

"Yes, they were and I can't *help* it."

Vee was trembling.

Anabel said, "All right. Calm down. I believe you." Then she snapped her fingers. "Wait a minute. That boy. Do you know a Mike Parsons?"

"He's a snoop," said Vee sullenly. "He listened outside the door."

"What door?"

"The classroom door when I was talking to the Provost."

"No, no," said Anabel. "That wasn't it. *He* told me that he saw the two of them—first your father, then Pat—hurrying out of the building. Now, wait a minute. It goes together."

"You said you believed me," Vee muttered.

Anabel shot her a withering glance. "You know, if you could leave yourself out of this, for two minutes . . . Did you think that Pat was *following* your dad? That your dad was trying to get away from Pat?"

"Maybe," said Vee.

"They were 'fighting'? That's what you thought?"

"Probably I was wrong." Vee was sullen.

"In your best judgment, they were fighting about *something?*"

Vee sniffled.

"You say they were running? You say Pat shouted? You say they drove off and went the wrong way?"

"They did," sniffled Vee.

"I wonder why," said Anabel. "I wonder why."

"I don't know why."

"Neither do I. Let's think about it." Then Anabel said, suddenly, "Thank you."

Vee got up and stumbled away.

She didn't belong here, Vee knew that. She'd just made a fool of herself. As usual. She huddled miserably in a big chair. Mrs. King was very nice and very kind to a stranger, but Vee was beyond that somehow. She needed more than kindness from a stranger. More than charity. Or maybe less. Something. Vee didn't know what.

Mrs. O'Shea wasn't very kind, really. Not like Mrs. King. She wasn't like Lillian, either. She was different. Vee shivered and summoned up resentment. Anabel. Well, Anabel was one of *those*. A lucky one. Always "in." Anabel's got a husband, and a baby, and her own house, and her own mother to come and help her. *She* doesn't know what it is to be all alone, with nowhere to go. So she doesn't care what she says to hurt somebody's feelings. She'll be sorry. . . . Vee tried to dream, but the mechanism had struck a snag. The dreaming process would not start. It had jammed.

About an hour later, Anabel took one more turn down the carpet on her long legs and said suddenly, "Come on, Vee. I'll take you over to get your things. Mother?"

Mrs. King said, "I'll take care of things here."

Vee had the sense of messages between them.

Anabel looked at the weather (which was dull again), dashed for the keys, her purse, and then into the hall closet for her coat. Then she stood and looked around her house with a kind of blank look. "I don't know what I might do."

"All right," Mrs. King said.

"Hurry up, Vee," said Anabel.

So Vee got out of the chair, feeling strangely bare in her rumpled dress.

When they were in the car, Anabel said, "Vee, if your father was trying to get away, and he didn't come home, where would he go?"

"I don't know."

"Maybe you do. At least, you'd know better than I."

"I don't know what you mean."

"Then listen," said Anabel. "If Pat was following your

father, then Pat would go where your father went. Your father would be leading. Don't you see that?"

"I guess so."

"Will you help me?"

"I can't imagine . . ."

"That's not what I'm asking you to do," said Anabel. "Or maybe I am. Let's us try to trace them."

"I don't see . . ."

"You know your father. You know this town. You must have been places with him. You'd know *something*."

Vee drew in her breath, ready to sniffle again.

"Listen," said Anabel, "what I want to go on is what you told me. Maybe you were right. They were fighting. I'm taking that for the truth. And I'm asking you to help me. Help your father, then. Help Pat. Won't you? At least you could try."

Vee felt queer. "I don't see how—"

"Never mind how," said Anabel. "You can't always see how. If you just try, then sometimes you can see how, as you go."

"All right," said Vee. "All right. I will."

"O.K.," said Anabel. "You didn't want to go to the hospital anyway." Anabel's sideways glance was challenging.

"No," said Vee, "I didn't." (It was true!)

"We'll get your stuff," said Anabel, in high spirits. "You need a coat. And then we'll try."

Cecil Wahl must have seen them park because he opened the door and looked out at them. Anabel said, "Hurry, Vee. I'll wait here. I doubt if you'll be raped."

"I'll hurry." Vee ran up the walk and in the door, past

him, and up the stairs. Of course she wouldn't be raped. What nonsense!

Cecil put a foot out on the porch, changed his mind, drew back into the foyer. He slipped the phone there from its cradle.

When Vee came pelting down again, with lipstick on crooked, wearing a clean dress, a light coat, and dragging her suitcase, he advanced to the bottom of the stairs and blocked her way.

"What's all this?" he said.

"Let me by."

"What's the hurry? Where are you going?"

"To find them." She looked him right in his green eyes. The eyes narrowed.

"What makes you think you can do that?"

"Never mind."

"Wait a minute. What have you heard?"

"Nothing. Nothing. But Mr. O'Shea was following Dad, and we think . . ." Vee's head was up.

"Oh, he was, was he? How do you know that?"

"I *saw* that."

"And you told her that?"

Vee said to him, boldly, "I don't always tell everybody everything I know. You'd just better let me by."

Cecil was looking up at her with shining eyes. "Well, well."

"And I could tell a little more, too," said Vee, "if you don't get out of my way."

Then he laughed. He slipped one arm around her waist and lifted her down the few remaining steps. Still embracing her, he swung her out the house door, firmed the door behind them, and hurried her down the walk, as gaily as if they were dancing.

Anabel, in the driver's seat, was leaning to hold the car door open. "Hop in," said Cecil. "You in the middle, Vee." Vee got in. She was panting. Cecil snatched her clumsy suitcase, tossed it over the seat into the back, got into the front himself and slammed the door. "What's the plan, girls?"

"We're going to try to trace them," Anabel said. "We don't need you."

"Maybe you do," said Cecil. "What do you mean? Tire tracks? Spoor, do you think? The bloodhound bit?"

"It'll take time. I'd rather not waste any." Anabel made the car move. "We can let you out at the first red light."

"Listen," said Cecil, "I want to find them just as much as you do. How are you going to proceed?"

"We'll see, as we go."

"But what if they call?"

"They won't call any sooner, for us agonizing by the telephone," said Anabel tartly.

He sank back upon the seat. His mouth seemed pursed to whistle but he made no sound.

"We can drop *you* any time," said Vee tightly.

"That's true," said Cecil softly. "That's very true."

Something made Anabel put her right hand on Vee's knee. She said, "We can try. You never know."

At this moment, for the first time since the storm, the sun came out.

In Vee's mind there was breaking, like Fourth of July spangles in the sky, a new vision.

Pat was sitting high against the headboard, shouting with

all the force he had in his lungs, "You go to the nearest house. You hear me, old lady? You tell somebody there's a sick man, needs a doctor. You go. Do that. And take your dog along." The dog raged in the other room. "Hear me? Am I getting through to you? Go on. Get going. Tell somebody. Otherwise, you'll have a corpse in this stinking bed and, sooner or later, the corpse will stink and what will you do then, old lady? Somebody's going to come and say 'It's O'Shea. O'Shea. O'Shea.' *Listen* to me. And get going."

She was standing by the door to the front room; all her wrinkles were turned downward.

"I'll help you," shouted Pat, "I told you that I would. But you've got to help me. Take your dog and your stick and walk to the nearest house. What is it? Half a mile? It won't kill you. But if you don't, it'll kill *me*. So go on. Hurry. *Get out of here*."

His good left hand caught at a pillow and ripped it from behind him and threw it. The old woman put up one claw. The pillow did her no harm.

Pat yelled, "All right. Then *I'll* go. Set the dog on. Let *him* kill me. I see no difference, old lady. Not anymore."

Her other claw turned the doorknob. She put her body into the yawn of the door, keeping the dog away. "Quiet, Rex. Down, Rex." She looked back at Pat. "No fear," she said.

Then the door closed and he was alone.

He listened. The dog's noises died away. Pat saw himself in the dusty glass over the old chest of drawers. Black clot on the side of his head, beard starting—he looked insane. He lay back and felt his entire frame quivering from his effort. Had she gone? Everything was still. He let his head loll. Damn it, he wasn't insane, but he was sick. He put his right hand to his chest, and chest, hand, leg, all of him, throbbed in one beating measure.

Not much longer, though. He closed his eyes. Wondered what time it was. Why he had been lying here so passively, with the old woman sitting on the chair, talking and talking? He had not listened. He seemed to know all about Johnny Pryde, even so. His mother's joy. A beamish boy. A paragon. Who wound up beating the boys, raping the girls, and worse. With the stubborn old woman, doting and blind . . . Pat could still hear her muttering voice, always with that latent cackle, that shrill strain, and that pounding repetition. It ran in his head like a tune, he'd be hearing it in his dreams.

" 'Wants his way. Wants his way.' That's what your pa says. 'Johnny wants his way.' I says, 'You never had your way,' I says to your pa. 'But Johnny shall have his way. He's a good boy, my boy. No fear.' 'Twelve years old,' your pa says, 'too young to run with them big kids.' But I says, 'No,' I says, 'Johnny Pryde, he's got no fear.' *I* told them kids. I says, 'You stay away from Johnny Pryde.' And they don't bother you. Eh, Johnny?" She cackled.

Pat opened his eyes. He wasn't dreaming. She was sitting there, in the chair. She hadn't gone anywhere. In her cracked mind, Johnny Pryde was just getting younger. Twelve years old and wants his way. *But doesn't get it,* thought Pat with a burst of light.

"Never," she said. "Never. No more."

He stirred. Then he saw that the dog was there, sitting beside her, mute, ready.

Her voice went on but Pat closed his eyes. Some other way, then. Outwit her. Use his brain. His brain went dart-

ing, this way and that. His body felt heavy and immovable.
"Anabel?" he said.

Anabel drove into the parking lot behind the Science
Building, turned solemnly all the way around, and headed
out again. Now, to the left. They would soon come to that
fork, where one could turn off toward the dormitories.
"Would Professor Adams go to the dormitories?" Anabel
asked the question aloud, but in her mind, she snatched at
an incomplete memory. There was some student about
whom Pat was very much concerned. What was the name?
Anyhow, there had been a theft and Pat felt that this boy
was being damaged by unjust suspicions. Could Everett
Adams have gone to accuse and Pat, angry, to defend this
boy? But what was his name? And did he room in the
dorm?

Before she could recollect anything about the name or
ask another question, Vee said, with finality, "They didn't
go that way. I would have seen them from where I was."

So Anabel drove on, toward the gym. After all, two
men, two cars, could scarcely be hidden anywhere near the
anthill that was the dormitory area. She brought herself
sharply to the problem of the next step and stopped beside
the tennis courts. There was only one court in use.

"Is it too dark for tennis by five-thirty? Maybe not to be
finishing a match. Better ask."

"I'll ask," said Vee, with unusual vigor.

Cecil opened the door and got out to let her out.

"Why don't you get in the back seat?" Anabel said to
him. He bowed. He got into the back seat.

The boy and girl on the tennis court had not been here,

Monday, and knew no one who had been. They stood still, staring after the car as it went on to the South West Gate.

There, Anabel stopped again. "If we go left, we only get back to the Main Gate and that makes no sense at all. So I say turn right, here. Agreed?"

"O.K.," said Vee.

"And you, Mr. Wahl, please watch to our left."

"What am I watching for?" He was irrepressibly amused.

"For a place where a car might have been wrecked and not easily seen. For a place where somebody is stationed who would naturally be watching the street."

"Such as?"

"Such as," said Anabel severely, "an old character in a rocking chair. An invalid in a window. A newsstand. Anything. And Vee, you watch to our right."

"I will, Mrs. O'Shea."

"Please call me Anabel."

They turned into traffic and went along. Just a street. A few scattering houses. Some vacant lots. Nothing to see. No one to ask. At the first intersection, Anabel stopped the car once more.

"Right, left, or straight ahead? Vee, do you know of any friend's house, any place at all—any reason for your father to turn here? One way or another?"

"To the right, is a dead end. It bumps into the campus. To the left . . . I don't know. I've never been." The girl was trying.

"We'll get into some fancy mathematics," said Anabel, "with so many alternatives. We can't explore every one."

"Not without," said Cecil, "our deerstalking caps."

Anabel turned around. "I am looking for my husband, Mr. Wahl. Vee is looking for her father. What are you looking for? Fun?"

"Please call me Cecil," he said sweetly, "and why are you so mad at me today?"

"No reason," said Anabel, conquering irritation. "I'm not." She looked straight ahead.

"Are *you* mad at me, Vee?" Cecil was being charming.

"Don't be so silly," said Vee. "What shall we do, Anabel?"

"We can't explore every way there is to turn," said Anabel, dismissing Cecil from her thoughts. "The only thing we have to go on is a tiny bit of probability. What do you think, Vee? Which way might your father go?"

The sun was shining. But Anabel had a gray feeling now. Which of them was silly?

Within the four walls of your own place, or inside the cave of your skull, you could scheme, dream. But when you got out into the world and the weather, it didn't work as you had dreamed it would.

But in a moment, Vee said, "Listen, sometimes if Dad wants to go to some store at the west end, he does take the next big street—you know?—and go back to town that way."

"Does he?" said Anabel. "All right, Vee."

She sent the car straight ahead. But she thought, Not back into town. How could two men, two cars, have vanished from the middle of town? She plodded along, looking to right and left herself—at a stand of tall grass where a man's body might lie, at a hedge, at a clump of shrubbery. Couldn't examine every one.

The most one could say for this expedition, it might beat sitting by the telephone. It might beat listening to the Provost's tenor coo, or people asking curious questions, or a police voice saying, "No, ma'am. Not yet."

She said, "I'd better call my mother every once in a while, in case anything has been found. Vee, what about *this* street?"

"I can't think of anything, Anabel."

Cecil kept quiet in the back seat. He was thinking that this expedition was typically square.

The car plodded on. At last, they came to a traffic light, where a major street crossed their path. Again, three choices. But there was a gas station here, and Anabel drove in, deep upon the pavement. They could ask. They could try.

A voice called, "Hi."

Vee answered, "Oh, hi, Dick."

The boy who walked over to them looked vaguely familiar to Anabel.

"Dick, you know my father, Professor Adams?" Vee was saying. "Did you happen to see him go by this corner, around five-thirty or six o'clock, Monday night?"

"No, I didn't," the boy said, with proper solemnity. "What's up, Vee?" But he was looking past her at Anabel. "Excuse me, but aren't you Mrs. O'Shea?"

"Yes, I am."

"I saw Mr. O'Shea," the boy said, "about that time."

Anabel's blood leapt. "Tell us," she cried. "They are missing. We are trying to trace them. So tell us every bit about it."

"Well, see, he was honking," the boy explained. "I was

washing a car, way back there. He honked real fast, you know? Like he wanted to say 'hello.' But he didn't see me. Looked more like he was trying to honk to some car ahead."

"A Chevy?" said Cecil quickly, from the back seat.

"I wouldn't know," said Dick Green. "Whatever car it was, it must have been pouring it on because Mr. O'Shea, *he* took the turn on about two wheels."

"Which way?" cried Anabel.

The boy pointed.

They left him with a babbling of thanks. Anabel's heart was singing. "Now we know they came this far," she cried. "They turned this way." She took her hand off the wheel and Vee's hand came up to touch it.

"So far, so good," said Cecil thoughtfully. "What's out this way?"

They didn't answer him.

Up in the pass, Maclaren and Carlson were standing at the side of the road, watching a slim uniformed man in high leather leggings who was walking up the steep mountain-side toward them, hauling himself hand over hand against a long rope that was snubbed around a rock and held at the brink by two of his colleagues.

"No lights," said a big Sheriff's Deputy who was in charge here. "Somebody saw the sun bouncing off the chrome. Fellow had some field glasses. So we get this report. You were looking for a Rambler. It's registered to Elihu O'Shea, 3407 Pine. That's your man, eh?"

"No body, you say?" said Carlson.

"Not in the car. But he could have crawled clear. Could have been thrown, too. Both doors open. So maybe he's someplace in the chaparral. Oh boy!"

Maclaren said, "Did I mention the windshield wipers?"

"He'll check. He'll check."

"Want me to go down?" said Carlson eagerly.

"You're not equipped." The big man looked at Carlson's trousered legs.

"Snakes?" said Carlson.

"Snakes? Oh man, there's a million of 'em. Poor S.O.B. Say he was hurt and crawled out. Before he gets a yard he coulda been bit and he coulda rolled on down."

"Service Detail coming?" asked Maclaren.

"Sure. Sure. Fingerprints. Bloodstains. What they can get out of it. Me, I got to organize this search, and what have I got here? A whole damn mountain, that's all. Just a whole damn mountain, crawling with rattlesnakes. It's going to take time."

Carlson crouched and peered over. The Rambler was almost invisible from the road. "Didn't burn, eh?"

"It musta flew," said the deputy. "What we kinda figure is, the fellow flew off the road in that big storm. That should be the size of it."

"So much for O'Shea, eh?" said Carlson.

"What was he doing up here in the pass?" murmured Maclaren.

"Not going to make much difference. He's just as dead," said Carlson. His gray eyes searched below. Maclaren stood still, looking up at the hills.

Finally, the man on the rope reached the brink and was helped over it. He dusted himself, panting. His colleagues in uniform and the two plainclothesmen waited respectfully until he had more breath.

"Keys are in it, ignition's on. Headlights off. Brake released. Windshield wipers are on."

"Good for you," said Maclaren heartily.

The man grinned at him. "And here's a funny one. Lever's in reverse."

"So what do you think?" The big deputy frowned. "Reverse?"

Carlson said, "Could the lever jolt into reverse when she rolled or hit?"

"Hard to say. I'd doubt it. If not, what was he doing? Trying to turn around?"

Maclaren said, "I'm wondering if he was in it at all."

"Listen," exploded the man, "if you can figure out some proof there was nobody *in* that thing when she went over, you'll be doing me one great big favor. A whole damn mountain, crawling with rattlesnakes."

"I wish I could do that."

The deputy grunted.

"Well," Maclaren said, "we'll go on up the road. See you, Harry."

"Right. Right. We'll *be* here, don't worry."

Carlson drove on up the mountain. His young face was frowning with thought.

"In case O'Shea went on up the road," said his partner, "there's a hamburger joint up here a little bit."

"Yeah, I remember it. O'Shea got missing Monday night. The big storm was Monday. About seven, seven-thirty?"

"We can check on that." Maclaren was respectful.

"So when he sent the car over, he forgot his wipers were on. Giving the time."

"*If* he did that."

"Who's going to be trying to turn around, in the dark and the rain, without lights?" said Carlson. "Looks pretty much as if he sent it over. Got rid of it. Took off."

Maclaren sighed.

"What's the matter now, Dad?" drawled Carlson, in a minute.

"You're jumping. First, he's dead, you're pretty sure. Now, you're pretty sure he's voluntarily disappeared. *But you don't know.* You don't know the man, for one thing. That's something to keep in mind."

"I'll remember," said Carlson blithely. "But if he did ditch the car and get lost, voluntarily, I was thinking about Mrs. O'Shea's ever-lovin' hero. A wife"—Carlson stopped and licked his upper lip—"could be wrong, I suppose."

"Anybody can be wrong," said Maclaren, shifting restlessly. "I'll have to call Mrs. O'Shea."

"Why? She's just going to get all upset and we don't *know* anything." The young man glanced sideways.

Maclaren said nothing.

"Yeah, I guess you promised," Carlson said. He frowned.

The first stroke of luck was the last stroke of luck they'd had.

Now they were getting into the country, going north slowly, slowly, corner by corner, stopping at every one. Anabel insisted. Anabel had gone to ring doorbells. It was people who cost them so much time, by not understanding what was wanted. Or by wanting to know the whole story before they would answer questions at all.

Anabel was thinking that it might have been smarter to put a notice in the newspapers, broadcast their questions by such public means, and let the information seek them out. It was plain that this expedition was bogging down. Vee was tiring, drooping. Couldn't stand up to repeated failures. Cecil was restless. Anabel had braced herself, long ago, to hear him begin to argue the futility of going any farther.

But Anabel dogged it and slogged it and went slowly, slowly, asking, watching, seeking—and failing. They might have, long ago, missed a turn, for all she knew. In fact, it was probable that they had.

One more, she thought. And then, One more.

She stopped the car again, and both her passengers sighed.

"How about here?" she said to Vee.

"Where is this?"

"Oleander Street." Anabel read the sign.

"Oh, yes," said Vee wearily. "We used to come out here. A long time ago. When I was just a little kid."

"Why was that?" Anabel made herself spark up.

"Oh, there used to be a place where you could dump stuff."

Cecil in the back seat said, "Dump?" There was something odd, drawling in the word. Skepticism, Anabel supposed. She was inclined to agree. How could this possibly be significant?

"Way out at the end there's a place," said Vee. "I used to ride out with Dad, and sometimes Mama, too." Vee's voice broke with fatigue and discouragement.

"Way out at the end? Maybe we'd better . . ."

Cecil said, "Listen, this poor child is starving. And so are we all. Why don't we go home now?"

"We better at least ask here." Anabel was hungry herself. "In the store. We could buy something to nibble on."

Cecil said, "They've got a phone, I see. Maybe you'd better call your mother?" He seemed to have livened up. He was full of ideas.

"All right," said Anabel. She pulled around the corner

into Oleander Street and parked. There was a delivery truck there and a boy was putting boxes into it.

Anabel would have spoken to the boy, from nothing but inertia, but Cecil cried, "Come on." He was out of the car and helping Vee out. "You don't know what you're doing anymore. You're punchy. Come *on*, Anabel."

So Anabel got out of the car. The three of them went into the little store. The boy looked after them.

It was crowded and dim, inside, with narrow aisles. Near the check-counter, an elderly man was putting up orders, holding a sheaf of them in one hand. He said, "What can I do for you?"

They were blinking in the changed light. Cecil said, "Phone?"

"Right over there."

"You go ahead, Anabel. How about a box of cookies, Vee? You have a carton of milk, sir?"

"In the case," said the grocer, gesturing. He went back to his work.

Anabel walked to the phone on the wall and began to hunt for a dime. She thought, Maybe I am getting so numb that I'm stupid. She knew that Cecil was picking a box from a shelf, and using his thumbnail on the dotted line to open it. She knew that Vee had stumbled to the refrigerated case and was opening it to get a wax carton of milk. She knew that the boy had come inside and was talking to the grocer. She felt her fingers tremble with fatigue as they pursued a coin. She did not listen to the voices.

"That's all for today, I guess, Mr. Johanneson?" Stan said. "I finished Martinez."

"Yep. That's it. I'm trying to get a head start on tomorrow. Say, Stan, can you make any sense out of this?"

Stan's young eyes had been noting, out of their corners, young Vee, sagging against the case, drinking her milk, looking kind of sad and kind of . . . well . . . mysterious. He brought his gaze to the paper in Mr. Johanneson's hand. "What's this?" he said.

"I'm asking *you*," the grocer said testily. "Posh something. Posh—what? What's she *want?* Polish? What am I supposed to send? Shoe polish? Furniture polish? Silver polish? Nail polish?" The grocer sputtered.

"Mrs. Pryde, eh?" said Stan. "Say, listen, has she got a license for that dog?"

"Why?"

"That dog is dangerous."

"Oh, go on."

"I'm telling you . . ." Stan said. He was stalling and he knew it. These strangers intrigued him.

Mr. Johanneson put the orders down. "Ask her when you see her—what she *wants*," he said irritably. "It's not going to make a lot of difference if she don't get to polish up something or other tomorrow. And you can tell her, she's got too much . . . Yes, sir?"

Cecil said, "How much?" He was selecting a cookie from the open package. "These, and the milk the young lady has."

The grocer peered at Vee and began to ring up the sale.

Anabel had found a dime and was dialing. There was no soundproof booth. The pay-phone hung on the wall. Over the space fell the silence that is embarrassing.

"Mother?" she said. All of them could hear.

Mr. Johanneson, wishing not to eavesdrop, snapped at Stan, "I said, that's it. You got a job to do. Do it."

Cecil turned to offer the cookies to Vee.

Then Anabel cried out, "Oh no!—Where? Where?"

Cecil dropped the cookie box on the counter and went racing toward her. Vee straightened and milk from the tipping carton in her limp hand dribbled on the floor. Stan was riveted where he was. Anabel, phone to ear, turned a wild and anguished face to the others. Cecil put the flat of his hand upon her back as if to hold her up. He bent his head to listen with her. Vee was paralyzed.

Mr. Johanneson did not like a disturbance. He needed his days to go evenly, as he had planned them. He had as much as he could do to manage that. He said to Stan, "Get along, will you?" So Stan tore his feet from the floor and went outside.

Anabel hung up. She wondered whether her heart was literally breaking. She put both hands up to hold it in.

Cecil said, in a caressing tone, "We'll go home. I'll drive. Try to take it easy, Anabel. They said there was nobody in it. I heard that. Come on, please. You're so exhausted. You've done everything you could . . ."

"But I don't think they know, for sure," said Anabel, resisting him as if he were the devil. "So we'll go up *there*," she cried.

"Oh no. Should you? Really?"

"Where else would I go except where Pat might be?" Anabel pulled away from him and ran toward the door.

Stan was still sitting in his truck as the three of them came running out. He craned his neck. He stretched his ears. The woman was white, but blazing with purpose.

The man was frowning. The girl was sobbing. They piled into the car, Anabel seizing the wheel in hands that were convulsively strong.

Stan yelled, "Hey, something wrong?"

Nobody answered him.

Anabel roared the Olds around in a U, and turned into the highway, going north. Could not wait to answer. The police had found the car. Need not wait to question. Their desperate and amateurish busy-work, time-wasting, useless expedition was over.

Mr. Johanneson had come out of the store to look after them.

"Hey, what was all that?" Stan called to him.

"Damned if I know," said Mr. Johnneson. "Fellow didn't pay for the stuff, even. Well, I guess they got trouble." Johanneson sighed. His heart was too soft, his brain knew it. Sometimes he sputtered or spoke too sharply, trying to protect himself from himself. He said, "Listen, Stan, maybe the dog is sick."

"Huh?"

"You didn't notice the meat order Mrs. Pryde's put in? That dog's going to live it up, looks like. Well, her budget won't stand for it, not more than this once. You'll tell her, tomorrow."

The strangers were far away now. Stan would never know what it was all about. He looked down at the grocer. "Hey, Mr. Johanneson, why doesn't somebody put the old witch in a home or something?"

"She's not doing any harm." The grocer was turning to go in.

"She's not all there, I'm telling you," Stan said.

"Listen, she hasn't been all there since Johnny Pryde went to the gas chamber. Let her be, poor soul." Johanneson's heart was soft; his conscience was quick. He said to Stan, "I don't mean you should take any chances with the dog, see? So . . . I mean take care of yourself."

"Oh, believe *me*," said Stan enthusiastically, "I won't bother *him*, Mr. Johanneson."

Anabel kept her mind on the driving, to go as fast as she safely could, to get through two towns and on, over the foothill slopes, into the pass and up the mountain. She wouldn't think about it. She would get there. She was grateful to Cecil for telling Vee the news, very briefly, and to Vee for sitting still and keeping quiet. She was grateful to them both for a companionable tension.

Having shaken out of town traffic, they raced up into the pass and Cecil said, "How will you know where?"

"I'll know."

It was easy to know. There were police cars, some kind of truck, many men. Anabel pulled up at the side of the road and set her brakes. As she opened the door, two men, whose faces were familiar, came quickly toward her. Maclaren said, "Just the car."

Anabel got out then, shakily. "It really is our car?"

"It didn't burn, Mrs. O'Shea. The registration."

"Where is it? Let me see."

"Down there." Maclaren began to guide her around the hood of the Oldsmobile to where she could look over. There was a car, far down, very far away, very small, and pitiful. It was a dead car; one knew that. Ours? thought

Anabel. With my sunglasses in the glove compartment?
And the maps from our trip? The hole where my high heel
gouges the mat? It was the death of a friend, in a way.

But Maclaren was looking over her head and he shouted,
"Watch her, Jimmy. The young lady."

Vee had slipped out at the other side and was peering
over the brink. Carlson scampered around the back of the
Olds on his lively young legs and caught her by the arm.
"You better get back in, Vi," he coaxed. "You don't want
to go sliding down there. Too many rattlesnakes. Come
on, Violet. Vee, I mean." He almost lifted the girl into the
front seat and stood between her and the brink.

Cecil, who had gotten out of the Olds and followed them
around the hood, said demandingly, "What's the official
version? What happened here?"

"One version," said Maclaren gently, "could be that the
Rambler stalled in the heavy storm and had to be abandoned. Somebody comes along, blind in the rain, hits it—
it goes over."

"With nobody in it?" Cecil asked.

"Nobody's in it now?" said Anabel. "You're sure?" She
leaned and Maclaren took her weight.

"Now, you know that we are sure," he chided.

"Yes, I . . . I believe you." Anabel was feeling confused.

"Come away." Motioning Cecil out of the path, he led
her to the other side of her mother's Olds, between the
traffic, which was the world going about its business, and
the vast, sad mountainside.

Cecil was leaning and peering. "Pretty far to crawl back
up to the road," he said crisply. "Could he have gotten out
at all?"

"Seems so," Carlson answered.

"He wouldn't get far."

Carlson said, "Hard to see what's in the brush."

"Watch it," said Maclaren. "Get her head down."

Carlson's strong hands began to bend Vee over, forcing her head toward her knees. But Vee said, "I'm all right. I'm all right. Don't do that."

"You're sure?"

"It doesn't *matter*."

She was struggling to sit up and he let her sit up, murmuring, "Take it easy." But she looked at him with a naked expression, devoid of any consciousness that she was a young female and he was a young male and that they had once encountered each other (or might have) in the high school jungle where the hunt is on. Every kind of defense or offense was peeled away. Carlson felt shocked. He said, "Shove over." He got in beside her and shut the car door. "She's just got the shakes a little bit," he said to the others in explanation. "She'll be O.K." He put his left arm around behind her. Pig or no, whatever . . . this poor kid!

But Vee wasn't even noticing. (Death was not romantic! It was terrible! It was awful! She didn't want *anybody* to be dead. Not Dad. Oh no, not poor Daddy! Not Mr. O'Shea. Please. Not even a stranger. Out here on the terrible mountain, alone. Alone. But what she wanted, or didn't want, would not matter. No dream of hers could change anything that was or had been. She had the shakes, yes.)

Maclaren said, "Are you all right, Mrs. O'Shea?"

"Yes." Anabel was numb, which was "all right" enough.

Cecil had come back to where they stood. "What makes

you think the Rambler might have been abandoned?" he demanded.

Maclaren answered, a little lamely, "That's only an idea. We don't know what really happened. But there's something else I think you'd better—"

"Go on," said Anabel forcefully.

"Sit down, Mrs. O'Shea?"

"No, just go on." Anabel had sensed, already, that there was more to be told.

"All right. If you don't mind," said Maclaren, and she received a strong impression that he was fond of her, that he was both respectful and affectionate, that he was on her side, "I'm going to tell you a little story." In his voice there was a promise. She was absolutely sure that he wasn't going to tell a story for nothing, that it would be important. They were all quiet, and Maclaren went on.

"Up the road," he said, "there's a small café. I called your mother from there, Mrs. O'Shea. My—er—partner was taking a cup of coffee. The man behind the counter told us this story. A funny thing, too.

"It seems, the night of the big storm—and that was Monday—lots of people took refuge in his place. There was a bus, for instance. Thirty or forty passengers crowded in. There were several cars that couldn't go on. The driving was terrible.

"Well, in the midst of the worst of the rain, a man came in alone. But he seemed to think he had a companion. When Mr. Mueller—that's the man we talked with—told him he'd seen nobody else come in, this fellow went to the door and looked out, as if he couldn't believe it.

"Well, he saw nobody. So he came and had coffee. And

when the rain stopped, everyone else went on his way except this one.

"He asked Mueller whether he'd ever watched certain TV programs," Maclaren continued. "The kind that . . . well, I guess you could say they flirt with the supernatural? He was pretty much shaken up by something, Mueller tells us. Finally, he said there had just been a miracle. He had to believe that his life had just been saved—by a ghost."

Strange, on the side of the mountain road, in the late daylight, with the traffic swishing by, and that knot of men so busy with their ropes, and their shouts to each other . . . strange, in this place, at this time, to be held and suspended, listening to a ghost story.

"It was the ghost," said Maclaren, "of a man in a shiny brown raincoat."

And Anabel's breath rushed into her.

"And a tannish rain hat."

Anabel smiled at him.

"It seems," said Maclaren, not missing her reactions but starting a flashback chapter, "this chap had been caught, on this road, going up in that downpour. He was driving alone. He was pretty scared. He didn't dare stop, for fear he'd be run into from the rear. But he hardly dared go on, either. He couldn't see. He said he prayed."

"Yes?" Anabel hung on the story.

"Then, suddenly, there was this figure on the road. Right about here, as far as we can judge. It was a man, in the shiny brown coat and the tannish hat. The motorist stopped and yelled to the man to get in and he asked if the man would please put his head out the right window and watch for the edge, while he himself with his head out the left window could just make out the white line.

"So the man in the raincoat did as he was asked. They crept along and they made it, to the café. It's only another mile. So the driver pulled up there, pretty glad and thankful. He said he'd buy his friend a cup of coffee, dashed through the rain. . . .

"But, you see, the man in the brown raincoat—just vanished."

Maclaren stopped and smiled, a little wistfully, at Anabel.

"Pat's raincoat is shiny brown," she said, "and he had it with him, and one of those limp plastic sou'westers in the pocket of it. A tannish color." She was feeling well and strong. The air was wonderful.

In the car, Vee whimpered, "But how could he vanish? What does he *mean?* Was it . . . Was it a real . . ."

"Ghost?" said Carlson. "Oh no, wait a minute."

Cecil snapped, "She asked a good question. How could he vanish?" Cecil was tense. He didn't seem to think that anything was amusing, at the moment.

"There was a bus," said Maclaren. "I mentioned that. We think it was a real man, but that, instead of following into the café, he spotted the bus standing there and boarded it and waited. And when the rain was over, the bus carried him away."

"Where?" barked Cecil. "Where was this bus headed?"

"Victorville, Barstow, Vegas, on to Salt Lake."

"So you're looking for . . . Wait a minute." Cecil seemed to grind his teeth. "I suppose you can turn up that bus driver?"

"Surely," said Maclaren. "I've already talked to him, in fact, on the phone." He paused. He seemed to be waiting for the next question. When no question came, he went on.

"He can't, unfortunately, confirm this guess. He says it is possible. He was in no mood to be counting heads. Felt he should be making up lost time and on wet roads. Then, when he got to his first rest-stop, he had to contend with his superiors. He might, or might not, remember a raincoat of that type or color getting off . . . somewhere."

Cecil Wahl was looking at Maclaren with narrowed green eyes. "I suppose you've found the haunted motorist, too?"

"No way to do that," said Maclaren. "No name given. Mueller didn't even see what he was driving."

And Cecil said, sunny with amusement now, "Be a shame, anyhow. Let him have his miracle. Change his whole life."

Anabel spoke, from a new and deep sense of trouble, "But Pat—would have called me."

"Oh look, honey," said Cecil, "he's *all right*, at least." He said to Maclaren, "I suppose you've got the word out for O'Shea in Victorville, Barstow and Las Vegas?"

"Surely."

"I don't understand this," said Anabel, standing straighter. "Did the . . . the ghost tell the motorist that his car had stalled? Or why he was on foot in the rain?"

"Not that Mueller was told, ma'am," said Maclaren, in soft sadness.

Carlson piped up, "Going to be tough to tell whether the car backed up a little too much or whether somebody just—"

Anabel whirled around and caught his young face with its mouth open, and his foot figuratively in it.

"Somebody just what?"

Vee Adams chimed in, "Somebody just what?"

Carlson's face smoothed out. "Sent it over," he answered

quietly. "Supposing somebody wanted to get rid of the car and just disappear."

"Why?" cried Anabel. "Why would he? Why?"

Nobody said anything until Vee spoke, in a shaky voice. "Where is . . . where is my father?"

And Carlson said quickly, as if he wanted to comfort her, "If he's down there, they'll find him."

She was right under his arm. He could feel the stab going into her. "But look," he tried to back water, "that's only . . . Nobody knows. Look, don't . . ."

Vee was not yielding to the sheltering pressure of his arm.

Anabel faced the other man. "Then they *are* looking for a body down there?"

"They have to do that," Maclaren said.

The air was cold. Anabel was freezing. "How soon will they be sure?"

"That will take time, Mrs. O'Shea. Reasonably sure? In the morning. To be absolutely sure might take days."

"Days?" It made her stagger.

"They've been trying to figure how to rig some lights," said Carlson, as if to be helpful with chatter. "But it doesn't look as if they can do too much without the daylight. Shadows can be pretty tricky." His voice died.

Anabel was bracing herself against the fact of a long uncertainty. "There is nothing we can do here," she said.

"No, Mrs. O'Shea."

"I'm sure you will tell me, as soon as they find anything. Whatever they find."

"I will, Mrs. O'Shea," Maclaren said, in his warm beautiful voice.

"That's right," said Carlson, rather humbly. "We promise."

Anabel said, "I don't understand this. I still say that Pat would have called me, no matter what, if he was able. But, maybe I should remind you"—she was holding her head proudly; the cold wind was cutting at her nape—"that Vee did think the two of them were fighting."

"Ah, did she?" said Maclaren. The music was deep and sad.

In the car, Vee lifted both hands as if to clutch the air and began to turn her head from side to side. Carlson's left hand came up to press her head against his jacket and stop that frantic motion.

Cecil, coming out of a stunned moment, cried, "Oh, Anabel. Look, Anabel, if something happened and your husband had to run away . . . it's none of *your* fault." (As if this might comfort her.)

"Fault!" she said, high and clear. "What an idiot you are! It would be my sorrow. It would cancel me."

She ducked her head and got into the car.

Cecil, quick as a cat to change his position, said, "I'm sorry. I'm sorry. I know. I know. Let me drive home, Anabel. Please."

She slid over to the middle as Carlson got out at the other side, seeming to prop Vee up against the seat as if she were a doll. There was some polite murmuring on Cecil's part.

Maclaren said nothing. His ugly face was sad.

The young man said nothing, but seemed to listen and watch and almost inhale every tiny impression.

Vee said nothing.

Anabel said nothing. She would trust to the truth and trust that she knew some of it. And if she were mistaken, then she would be canceled. If Pat had done some terrible deed and run away, then she would have to start all over again, and from the bottom. But not yet. Not yet. Not yet.

They drove all the way back to Riverside without a word spoken.

When they were well into that town, Cecil said apologetically, "Do you think you could get home all right, if I stop to see my sister?"

Anabel said, "Of course."

So they went on to the hospital and stopped. Cecil sat a moment, sliding his hands up and down, up and down, on the steering wheel, as if he were trying to frame something to say. At last, he sighed and got out. "Coming, Vee?"

Vee began to fumble at the latch of the door. Then she twisted to reach over into the tonneau for her suitcase.

"Let it ride with me," said Anabel. "I won't wait. But we'll wait supper."

"Am I supposed," gasped Vee, "to stay with you, *now?*"

"Don't be silly." Anabel's lips felt numb.

Vee said quickly, "Then I'm going home with Anabel. I don't need to see Celia."

Cecil was on some kind of tiptoe, as if he were held to earth by the merest thread, as if he could fly. Yet he was tethered. He didn't seem to know what to do, what to say, whether to argue with this decision or not.

Anabel said, "Thank you for . . ." She didn't go on. She'd lost her phrase. Wasn't in the mood for polite murmuring.

Cecil lifted one hand, as if to reject any thanks, but

then, irrepressibly, the gesture became a gay flip that said "So long." He loped away toward the entrance.

Up on the mountain, it was beginning to get dark. Carlson said, "If you want a theory, *why* he would send the car over, you can say maybe he did have a body in it. Say they did fight. O'Shea doesn't know his own strength or something. He panics, afterwards." The young man glanced at his partner. "This is just a theory. There may be a couple of things we don't know yet. Right?"

"In that case, where's the other car?" Maclaren brooded.

"Oh. Yeah. The Adams car." Carlson walked restlessly away to look over the brink where the work was ceasing with the falling darkness. It was as if he thought there might be two cars down there and meant to check. Rooted on his two tall muscular legs, he stood. Maclaren tilted his ugly head, as if fondly.

Cecil came swiftly into the hospital room, cast one glance at the other bed, which was rumpled but empty of its occupant, and bent over his sister. "What does Vee know? I better have it. And fast." He was on tiptoe, to be gone.

Celia was looking better. Very beautiful, with her pale hair drawn cleanly back and tied up in a ribbon. Her color was better. She lay on the high bed with the white covering pulled tightly and smoothly around her as if she had not moved since she had been tucked in. She did not move now.

He straightened. "Just checking," he said distantly.

"No, no," she said. "Nothing."

"She doesn't know, for instance, about the night the fat man . . ."

"Impossible."

"Tell me how it's impossible."

His sister lifted her head, looking strained and uncomfortable. "Because Ev told me, about a hundred times, not to let her know. Because he kept saying she was too young to 'understand.' What do you want, C? What's the matter?"

"So the kid's got ears. She overheard."

"She did not. She wasn't even in the house. Not one word was said in the house while she was there."

"Then what's she hinting about?"

"Who knows? She's just a moony little kid, C. Who's going to pay any attention to her, for pity's sakes?"

He sagged a little and his mouth pursed to whistle. "It was a long day I had for nothing, then."

"What?"

"Where's your . . ." He jerked his head, indicating the other bed.

"Walking around. She's going home tomorrow. Not soon enough for me," said Celia viciously. "Did Ev call?"

He eyed her and his lids winced. "I wasn't around. But it was just as well I went with them, I guess." He told her quickly what had been found on the mountain.

Celia lay, still as a mummy.

"Listen, C," her brother rushed on. "The man in the raincoat must have been our Ev. *We* know it couldn't have been O'Shea. Although what the devil Ev was doing in O'Shea's car . . . Never mind. Right now, the cops are looking for O'Shea along that bus route. So far, so good. But the minute they pick up Ev . . ."

"They'd better not pick up Ev, then," she said sullenly.

He blew out breath. "You still think I can fix it?"

"*I* can't. I would if I could."

Green eyes spoke to green eyes. Her mouth quirked. "Oh sure. When I'm sick. When you can't take *me* . . ."

He shifted his weight.

"Too bad," she said listlessly. "I'd get half. If you could fix it. And I'll get well. We could . . ."

"I'd get better than that," said her brother. "Off the hook. O.K. Let's say I would, if I could, too. O'Shea's no problem. The problem is, where's Ev?" He rubbed his head.

She began to walk her fingers on the smooth band where the sheet was turned over the spread. She was smiling, faintly.

He said, "Listen, Vee did this sort of thing all day. You try it, C. Where would Ev go? You know him. Try and think. Must have been chance that he got on that particular bus for Victorville, Barstow, Vegas, Salt Lake. Wait, you took that crazy honeymoon up that way."

"The cure, you mean?" she said bitterly. "Good old Bedelia's? Two and a half months. In a motel. A mo-tel."

"He wouldn't go where he'd be known. Or would he?" Cecil was jittery.

"Why worry?" she said. "You'll find out when he telephones."

He didn't speak but she read his mind. "You know why he didn't, don't you?" she cried. "He's waiting for me. Probably hasn't got the faintest notion that I don't know where he *is*, the old fool. So. He'll wait until tomorrow, late, when I don't show."

Cecil said softly, "That may be, but you *don't* know where he is. And neither do I."

"There's time."

"Time for what, C?"

"You should have a car, ready to go. The minute he calls—"

"Where will I get a car?"

"Rent?"

"No license."

"Borrow?"

"From whom? Anabel? Not a chance."

"Mrs. Newcomb? Next door?"

"Old curiosity shop?"

"You could, C."

"And I'm a sitting duck," he said, "until some time late tomorrow?"

"They're looking for O'Shea, you said."

"And suppose they find O'Shea? That body will turn up. Right then, the cops are looking for Ev. And I'm not crossing their path."

"But the cops are wrong."

"Looking for the wrong man? That's what I said."

"They're looking in the wrong *place*," she said fiercely, "Don't be stupid, C."

He cocked an eyebrow.

"They're looking for a body on the mountain, you said. But Ev left the body at some dump or other. He told me. I told you. Why will they find it tomorrow if they haven't found it yet? Maybe Ev buried it."

Cecil said nothing but she heard the inaudible click in his mind. "What?" she demanded. "What?"

He rubbed his head. "I've got a hunch that I know where this dump *is*. That's a funny thing."

Her head lifted. Her eyes shone.

"I don't mind taking a bit of a chance," he said, "but this is ridiculous." His eyes were merry.

"There's time," she insisted.

"For what, C?"

"For *you* to bury O'Shea."

"For what reason?" he drawled.

"For *time*. Time to keep the cops looking for *him*. Until Ev calls."

"So I bury one body and what do I do with the other one?"

"What one?"

"Ev's."

She shrugged. She closed her eyes. "What will you do with *yourself?*" she inquired listlessly. "Otherwise?"

"Be a little bit careful," he said and her eyes popped open. "Don't pressure me. I can start in two minutes." He shrugged. "From now."

She said, drearily, "When I'm sick . . ."

His eyes were cold. "You are sick, C."

She said, "Then, they'll be asking *me*, won't they? Where would your brother go? You know him. Try and think."

The telepathy between them was very strong. He winced and chewed his lip.

Then Celia's roommate came walking in, wearing a long maroon robe of surpassing ugliness. "Well, hi!" she boomed. "Company, I see. Say, are you two *twins?*"

"Yes, ma'am," said Cecil. Then he touched his sister's cheek lightly. "I'd better . . ."

"Get on with it?" she murmured.

"I'll see, C."

"Shall I wait, then?"

On his face broke the irrepressible mischief. "Why don't you take a bit of a chance?" he said teasingly. The cobweb that tethered him broke and he was gone.

The roommate was letting her chunkiness down upon the other bed. "Must be real strange to be a twin," she said. "Real strange, you know?"

"I know," said Celia. Her mouth twisted. She turned her cheek to the mattress and folded her pillow over her upper ear.

"O.K., little sunshine," grumbled the roommate.

The Provost was an unhappy man. He had forbidden his wife to discuss the matter at the dinner table, but afterwards he had retreated into his study, pleading work to do because he simply could not discuss anything else, and her obedient chatter seemed fantastically irrelevant.

At about nine o'clock, he had called his friend—by now the Provost and Captain Murch were old buddies—only to be told once more that there had been no developments and probably would not be until morning.

But the Provost knew that he had a responsibility. He must say what he could to poor Mrs. O'Shea. He had put off calling her. He had told himself that he had been hoping for better news.

But now, at about 9:30—when it would soon be too late for an evening phone call—he found her number and braced himself.

A woman answered. She said she was Mrs. O'Shea's mother.

The Provost exerted himself to be very very happy

that Mrs. O'Shea was not alone during this trying time. Then Anabel came to the phone.

He stated his concern, he spoke of not giving up hope, he spoke of her courage. She seemed calm, he thought, and he was glad of that. He went on to something else that was bothering him.

"You must realize, Mrs. O'Shea, that the newspapers are going to report the—er—accident in tomorrow's editions and I think perhaps you should be prepared to—"

"They've been here," she told him.

"Oh, indeed? Already? I . . . rather hope that you did not—er—say very much about Professor Adams having also chosen this moment—"

"They know about that."

"Oh, me," said the Provost, "I *am* sorry."

"I'm not," said Mrs. O'Shea. "Somebody may read about it who knows something and can tell us."

"Oh, me. I had hoped . . . I spoke to Mike Parsons, you see, and I did hope that I had done something to squelch . . . You did not discuss that reckless speculation?" He was worried and he was a little sharp.

She said, "No, but I can't worry about it, Mr. Drinkwater."

"I understand," he said (which was the truth). "Please believe that I couldn't be sorrier for this tragic accident."

"Accident?"

"Why, that your husband's car went off the road in that cloudburst. A terrible thing! A very terrible—"

"Mr. Drinkwater, don't you know about the man who was picked up? In the brown raincoat?"

"Oh, yes, of course. But I am very much afraid that it was just some hitchhiker . . ."

The Provost checked himself. He was not really a brutal man. He had human compassion. He was truly sorry for this poor young wife. He was inclined to believe, with her, that only tragedy explained the events. Still, he ought not to argue, to her, that her husband was dead, by accident, on that mountain. Even though this was, in his view, not the best, not the happiest, not the most desirable solution, but the simplest, certainly. A simple accident in an automobile. Tragic loss of a bright young man. And a "nine days' wonder."

The Provost was fond of declaring, at dinner parties, his unchecked theory about the origin of that phrase. He would say, twinkling, that a "nine days' wonder" was actually the observation of a truth, made by generations of the folk. Empirical knowledge. Nine days was the exact time it took for news to become stale.

He thought, now, that a tragic accident was of course tragic, but after nine days, it would be forgotten by everyone—except Mrs. O'Shea, naturally.

"I can be wrong," he said compassionately.

Anabel said, "You still think that Professor Adams has nothing to do with this?"

"I do tend to think so. By the way, I—er—"

"And you also tend to think," she said—now he heard her voice pick up vehemence and sparkle—"that although a man was on the road, just about where the car went off, wearing a raincoat the color of Pat's raincoat and a rain hat the color of Pat's rain hat, *he* has nothing to do with it, either?"

The Provost said, "I would say, probably—"

"As a mathematician's wife," said Anabel tartly, "I know about probability."

"Ah," said the Provost, piqued, "and isn't it very prob-able that, in the rain, most men wear raincoats?" He was ashamed of himself immediately. "Please forgive me," he cried. "I certainly don't mean to quibble in the face of this very tragic. . . . You must continue to be as courageous as you . . ."

"Courageous enough," she said, "to have thought of the hitchhiker."

"Now, my dear . . ."

"My hypothetical hitchhiker," said Anabel, "who, if he stole the car, stole the raincoat right along with it. Which, I have to admit, would explain to me why the man-in-the-raincoat did not go into the café, where there was a tele-phone, and call me."

The Provost felt shocked. When he'd spoken of courage he had not meant anything like this. He had had in mind a certain womanly patience and restraint. "You must not think—" he began.

"Oh, yes, I must," snapped Anabel.

"We must wait," he said piously but rather rapidly, "and hope. I have not been able to get in touch with Mrs. Adams. I am wondering . . ." He was anxious to change the sub-ject. He felt he needed no additional taste of Anabel O'Shea's temper. Although she astonished him, and also touched, somehow, a buried nerve that was not quite dead yet.

"Mrs. Adams is in the hospital," she told him. "An ap-pendectomy. Last evening. She is all right."

"Indeed? Thank you, very much. But the daughter . . ."

"She is here, with me."

"Oh, indeed. Well, I am very happy to hear that." The Provost didn't know whether he was happy or not. He was surprised. "I wonder if I could speak to her, please?"

"Of course."

"And we will all hope and pray . . ." The Provost did not go on with this sentiment, because he seemed to know that Anabel was no longer holding the other phone to her ear.

Vee's voice said, "Mr. Drinkwater?"

"My dear Violet." He warmed up his voice. "I am so glad to have discovered where you are. I have been worried about you. Are you all right?"

"I'm all right, I guess."

"No news yet about your father. Too bad. Too bad. I didn't know that your mother was ill, my dear. I have called your number several times during the day, but there was always the busy signal. Well! It's good to hear your voice. Please try not to worry too much, and if there is anything *I* can do, remember."

"Thank you."

"I am very glad that you are not alone."

"So am I." Her voice was fading.

"Then, good night," he said caressingly. "You are a very brave girl." He hung up. He felt he had done passably well with her, at least. But he was not a happy man.

Mrs. King was mending a rag doll for little Sue, who was sound asleep abed at this hour. She looked up from the work and exclaimed, "What is it?" Her hands put the work aside. "Why, child, you look as if you've seen a ghost!" Mrs. King began to wiggle out of her chair.

Anabel whirled and saw Vee, hanging onto the back of the sofa.

They had not said much to each other during this strange

evening. Anabel had not discussed with the girl the proposition that Anabel's husband might have sent this girl's father over the mountain to his death. Anabel would have been glad to proclaim her own conviction that this had not happened, but even to deny it would have raised the question. Furthermore, it would have raised the question of Anabel's hypothetical and vicious hitchhiker, to which horror she had not wanted to give any more substance than it already had in her mind. So the miserable girl had simply been here, in the house, and Anabel's mother had created what ease she could.

But now, Anabel, having just been forthright with the Provost and found it a relief, too, sent herself swiftly across the carpet.

"Anabel?" said Vee pitifully.

"All right. Whatever it is. I'm listening."

"My father must be home."

"What do you mean?"

"Because"—Vee swallowed—"the Provost said . . ." She looked scared.

So Anabel touched her. "Just tell."

"The Provost said he called our house several times and always got a busy signal."

"Yes?"

"But there wasn't anybody home." Vee struck her hands together. "So how *could* there be a busy signal?"

Anabel had been expecting a blow, somehow. Now she felt her brain snatch up the point. "That's right," she said. "Your stepmother's in the hospital. Cecil was with us, almost all day. I see. I see."

Color flooded into Vee's face.

But Mrs. King said, "Oh, my dears, that doesn't neces-
sarily . . . Think how this phone has been ringing. I do
believe that if two calls are trying to come in at once, one
of them gets a busy signal."

"Ye-es," said Anabel. "I think so. But . . . He did say
several times?"

"Yes, he did."

Anabel said, "I don't know. You might as well figure
that the Provost laid it on a little thick. Maybe he called
once. People will do that."

"I know it," said Vee. Then she burst out, as if she had
found new courage to speak up. "But the thing is—Anabel, you keep saying that Mr. O'Shea would call you. Well,
my father . . . It's the same thing. He's so crazy about
her. He would call Celia, if he could. Not *me*. I know that.
But he just couldn't keep away from *her*, if he's alive.
So, maybe he has been calling. Or else, come home."

Anabel said gravely, "You know, I think you are right."
She went to the phone. "What is your number?"

Vee gave it to her. Vee's cheeks seemed to have lost some
of the childish plumpness. Vee's eyes were not now sliding
or evading. She was not being demure. She was gazing at
Anabel and Anabel knew that Vee was in the process, and
had been for some time, of making herself a new crush, a
new idol.

Anabel did not especially want to be anybody's idol.
She turned her attention to her dialing. No answer at the
Adams house. But no busy signal, either. "Hm." Anabel
wiggled one foot on the ankle. "Cecil may still be at the
hospital, I suppose. But it's late."

"Maybe when he got home, Dad was *there*, and they
both went to see Celia?" Vee was breathless.

"Hm." Anabel wiggled her eyebrows. "That could be, too." She found the number of the hospital.

"Mrs. Adams, please? What's her room number, Vee?"

"I don't know, but the fourth floor . . ."

"On the fourth floor," said Anabel.

"We have no way of connecting you with a patient, after nine P.M.," the voice said, pleasantly enough.

"How can I find out . . ."

"I'll connect you with the floor nurse."

The new voice was annoyed. "We *cannot* permit a *patient* to take a *phone call*, after nine P.M."

"Yes, but—"

"Mrs. Adams is doing very well. You may call her in the morning."

"Just a minute," said Anabel. "Is Professor Adams there?"

"No visitors now. Too late."

"Has he *been* there?"

"I really couldn't say."

"Has he *phoned* there, then?"

"It's too late," the voice snapped. "We cannot have the patients upset. Or disturbed."

Then Anabel sat with a dead phone in her hand.

She got up and took a few turns up and down the room. "I wonder . . . They could be on their way back to your house."

"Or else," said Vee, "the neighbors might have seen Dad. If he did come . . . If he is home . . ." Then Vee Adams smiled, with a peculiar sweetness. "It might not have anything to do with you, Anabel."

"I could bear to know," said Anabel. "Shall we go?"

Vee gasped and went running to the coat closet.

The Adams house was dark. Anabel parked at the curb and peered out at it, leaning across Vee, who said, "They're not there now, I guess. Shall we get out, Anabel?"

"Well, we're not going quietly. What's the best place to ask?"

"Mrs. Newcomb," said Vee promptly.

Mrs. Newcomb put on her porch light before she opened her front door. "Why, Violet!" she cried. "You poor dear child! Come in. Come in."

Vee said, "We just came to ask you . . ."

But Mrs. Newcomb went right on talking. "Your . . . er . . . I mean Mr. Wahl, only just *told* me that you were with a friend. I've been wondering where you'd got to. How *is* your mother? I called this morning and they said she had come through just splendidly. Won't you come in?" This woman had a long nose and little eyes, set close. "Both of you?" she simpered. She made the question, Who is this?

"This is Mrs. O'Shea," said Vee, rather helplessly.

"Mrs. Newcomb," said Anabel briskly, "have you seen Professor Adams?"

"No, but I've talked to him," the woman said. "Come in, do."

"Wait a minute. You say you've *talked* to him? When was that?"

"Why, just a little while ago. Poor man. Imagine, not even knowing that his own wife had been taken to the hospital in an ambulance. Imagine, *my* having to be the one to tell him." Her lively little eyes reproached the daughter. "So strange. Of course, I was glad to do it."

"This is important," said Anabel. "Has he gone there?"

"To the hospital? Well, I couldn't say, of course. But I think he had intended to phone there. As a matter of fact, he asked me to find the number for him. Won't you come in? No one's at your house, Violet. I let Mr. Wahl take my car, you know. He had some important errand and taxi's are so inconvénient. I was glad to do it. I'm sure he is perfectly reliable."

Anabel said, "You didn't see Everett Adams, then? You talked to him on the phone?"

"Why, yes, I thought I had said—"

"Your phone?"

"Well, no. You see . . . Poor Mr. Wahl. All this trouble on his shoulders. His poor sister. And then the Professor being out of town and nobody able to get in touch with him. Or so I assume." Mrs. Newcomb tossed her head. "After he had left, it occurred to me . . . I thought it would be only neighborly. And I have always been a good neighbor—"

"You went to my house?" Vee burst.

"You know," said Mrs. Newcomb accusingly, "that your back door can be opened. I did think I might just look around. Perhaps I could lend a woman's hand, to straighten up the place a bit." Her nostrils pinched.

There was no speeding her up. Anabel nerved herself to wait.

"Well, I went over. And do you know, I noticed that someone had carelessly left the phone off the hook? Naturally, I replaced it. And the Professor must have been trying to get the number all along, because I hadn't been in the house ten minutes before he called!" She nodded, as if pleased about this.

"Well, when he asked for Celia, you know I was quite

shocked. Fortunately, I was able to tell him that she had come through the operation just splendidly." The woman beamed and nodded as if she congratulated herself.

"This was how long ago?" Anabel asked.

"Why, I can't say—exactly." The woman peered at her suspiciously. "Oh, half an hour, something like that."

"From where was he calling?"

"Why, I don't believe . . . As a matter of fact, he didn't *say*. He was very much upset, you know. Naturally. Do come in."

"Thank you. No," said Anabel, with decision. She took Vee's arm and hurried her away. Mrs. Newcomb, taking obvious offense, stood on her lighted porch and openly, and rather hostilely, watched them scurry to the Adams' door.

Vee had her key. They went in and turned up a light. Anabel was looking at the phone in the foyer. It was as if she spit on her hands.

"This is Anabel O'Shea again."

"Yes?"

"Did Mrs. Adams get a phone call from her husband this evening?"

"There are no phones in the patient's rooms, after nine P.M." The starched voice indicated dutiful patience.

"All right. Did he *try* to call? Who would speak to him? Would you?"

"All I can tell you is that we do *not* permit calls to *any* patient, after nine P.M., and that is an inflexible rule. I *cannot* and I *will not* break it. Not *tonight* or *any* night." The patience was exhausted.

"Don't you hang up!" Anabel was sharp. "This is a police matter."

"Are *you* the police, madam?"

"No, I am not."

"Then why don't you call the police?" Starched voice was skeptical.

"I intend to. What is your name, please?"

"More. *Miss* More." Starched voice was proud of it.

Anabel hung up. "I think he did call. I think he did. She's just too ornery to say so." Anabel snatched up the phone again, and in a little while was talking to Captain Murch himself on a special line.

When she hung up this time, Anabel sat still, wondering what more there was that she could do. Nothing—about Everett Adams. The police would check on him now. He had either called the hospital or he had not. The police would either find out where he was or they would not. The chance that he would know where Pat was seemed remote. But surely Everett Adams wasn't on the mountain. It was Pat's car, Pat's coat, Pat's hat . . . And in Anabel's imagination a ghost, in a brown raincoat, hitched rides. She let the pang go through her.

Then she sighed and looked around. This house was drab and chilly and foreign. What was she doing here?

"I'm sorry, Vee," said Anabel, "I guess I'm just the bossy type. I shouldn't have taken over like that. But at least you know that your father's alive and evidently well." Anabel tried to smile.

But the girl was looking white and strained and she was watching Anabel intently.

Anabel rose. "Do you want to stay here, in case he tries to call you?"

"He won't," said Vee, in a low intense voice. "He doesn't even remember me."

Oh no, sighed Anabel in herself, as if I haven't got my own troubles. She said, "Well, that's up to you. I guess there's no point in our going to the hospital. Unless *you* want to go there. If so, I'll take you."

"No," said Vee in the same manner. "Celia doesn't want to see me. She doesn't care."

"All right," said Anabel mildly. "We'll go home, then, I suppose."

"I don't know what to do," Vee wailed.

"And I can't tell you," said Anabel, rather severely, "but I'd suggest you come with me. I wouldn't think there was anything more that either of us can do tonight. Tomorrow . . ." She started for the door. (Tomorrow they would search the mountain.) She turned to hurry up the girl.

Vee stood with her head hanging, in that attitude of distress.

Anabel said, "Oh, come on. This just isn't the time to worry about who cares for you and who doesn't. In fact, you could cheer up a little. You were pretty sharp about the telephone."

Vee lifted her head and gave her a strange look, a shaky smile. Then Vee stumbled out the door. It was Anabel who turned the lights out. She was frightened and very weary from having been frightened for so long. It did cross her mind to wonder who had left that telephone off the hook. But it didn't seem to matter.

Going home, she was grateful for Vee's silence.

"So I guess you better get on over there," said Captain Murch to Carlson on the phone, "and get hold of this Miss More and get it out of her, whether Adams already phoned there. If he shows up, you grab him. Don't worry about a thing. I want to know where he's been and what he knows."

"Yes, sir."

"And if he hasn't phoned there yet, you may have to stick around until he does. You can let his wife do the talking, but be sure you find out where the hell he is."

"Yes, sir."

Wednesday Night

Pat said, "For better or for worse. Stand up and you say it. Why? Because she's such a sweetheart, you can't stand it. You gotta get married. *Ev*-vrybody has to say that. Don't know what you're in for."

The lamp gave a flickering light.

The old woman said, "A real strong constitution. Your pa was the weevily one. Not my side. Healthy, all the Mayhews. Your Grandma Mayhew, she was ninety-nine when she passed on. She used to say, she says to me . . ."

The air was very dry.

Pat said, "Then there's a day and the next day and a week and the next week, a year and the next year. This Anabel turns out to be quite a dame. You didn't know the half of it. Tell *me* it's just the old rat race, the job, the bills, the baby. I don't know . . ."

The bed was hot.

The old woman said, " 'Estrella,' she says to me, 'you're a Mayhew and Johnny's a Mayhew, too. I can tell,' she says. She's ninety-six or ninety-seven, that time, and you was only four years old, Johnny. She was blind by then, too.

Well, she was old. But she put her fingers on your little face. 'He's a Mayhew,' she says. 'No fear.' "

Pat said, ". . . what they think life's made of. Sugar and spice and all things nice, like the job and the bills and the baby . . . and Anabel. That ain't no rat race. That's my life. My wife. She's not going to sit in the corner and cry for me. No sir. No ma'am. In sickness or in health . . ."

The dog barked.

The old woman said, "A little touch of the influenza. That don't bother me. Ninety-nine, she was, when she passed on and I'll be, too. And so will you, Johnny Pryde."

She cackled.

Pat said, "Because this kid's not what you'd call the passive type. I ought to know. And I pity the world. I really do. Be turning it upside down. So long as we both shall live."

He rolled his head. The air was dry and still. The lamp was sputtering. The dog was barking.

"Eh, Rex?" he shouted.

The old woman said, "Eh? Eh, Rex?" She got up, using her staff, and went to the bedroom door. She looked back over her shoulder. Pat lay hunched up, his eyes squirrel-bright, shrewd, and a little mad, with fever.

Grumbling to herself, the old woman came back and picked up the lamp. She took it with her. Long shadows wavered up the walls. She left him.

Cecil was holding Mrs. Newcomb's flashlight close to his body, directing the light almost straight down. He was well within the grove now, following some ruts, along which he had not dared drive Mrs. Newcomb's Ford. He had left it at the end of Oleander Street, but well away from where, muffled in neglected shrubbery, there was a house with a dim light in it.

Surely no one could hear his feet on this still-soaked, mushy ground, and no one would notice his light if he were very careful. He dared send the beam a little farther ahead and it seemed to leap, as if suddenly nothing obstructed its range.

He turned it downward and went on, very gingerly, until he came to the end of the ground. There was a cut in the earth. A drop. Cecil shuffled sideways and found a tree trunk to which he clung with his left arm. Then he sent the beam of light down over the edge. A dump, all right. There was the old shoe, the inevitable one old shoe. There was a rusty gallon tin, from some nursery. There were heaps of ancient weeds and cuttings. There was a tire. The tire was on a wheel. The wheel was on a car. The car was upside down. It was Everett Adams' car.

The flashlight's beam trembled over its somehow indecently exposed underparts. No way to see from here, at night, whether there was anybody in the car. But that was where he was, all right. O'Shea.

Cecil, seized by the notion that he had no idea what might be watching him from the other side of this gulch, slid the button and the dark became seamless. It was so silent here. All sound was distant. Close by, one seemed to be able to hear the rotting process. The sweet smell of decay came up to his nostrils. He let go of the tree and turned around. He could glimpse that faint light in the house. It must guide him. Cecil began to hurry, shuffling in order not to stumble, anxious to get away from here, especially since, somewhere, a dog was barking.

He had his left arm stiff before him, to guard against bumping into anything. He began to fumble with his right thumb to slide the flashlight button and give his feet some light and hurry on.

But light became greater over there, around the house. And the dog was louder. But Cecil could see the grayish look of the open road, beyond the grove. He began to run, fearing that the dog was out of the house. He slipped and threw up his right arm for balance. The flashlight fell out of his hand. The dog was out. Cecil did not fall. He kept his feet, his feet raced, he made it.

Then he was panting, inside the glass and metal fortress of the car. He turned the key, pulled the lever and, without lights, he backed the car and turned it around.

The dog raced on the road behind him, swift and silent. But not as swift as he, as he drove away from Oleander Street.

Pat heard the racket of a car starting up in the night, the motor racing. Then he heard the sound diminish as it went away. He had not heard it come. He was leaning on his left elbow. His right arm was beginning to swell up. He heard the old woman shrieking for the dog and he heard the dog's return.

And he thought, as he heard the house door closing, She'll bury me. She'll put up a stone. The stone will say *Johnny Pryde*.

The whole bed seemed to tilt. He started to count. Count something. Anything. The hours. He didn't know this hour. The days, then. Monday, Tuesday, Wednesday . . . This must be Wednesday night. . . .

Wednesday night.

Jamie Montero was lying the wrong way on his bed, with his head where his feet ought to be. This way, he could look out the window at the pool of light under the high streetlamp. He'd lain this way two nights in a row, already. This night, he saw the Ford go by, very fast. He had seen it before. Now he saw it coming back. He checked it off. It wasn't a two-toned Chevy. The driver probably just hadn't known this was a dead-end street.

But that was the trouble. Oleander Street went nowhere. So where was that Chevy? Jamie was sure he hadn't missed it Monday night. Nor Tuesday night either. By day, he had taken little naps in his chair, but he'd had the little kids watching the street for him by day. And the Chevy had *not* come back. Where was it then? Stan hadn't helped very much. Stan, the grocery boy, was nice and all that, but maybe he wasn't serious. He was too old to be serious, really. But the little kids, who knew how to be serious, wouldn't go out to the end to look around, not even for Jamie. They were too scared of the old witch and her dog. Jamie sighed. He wasn't scared, but he couldn't go.

Wednesday night.

The Newcomb house was dark. Cecil Wahl ran the Ford into the Adams' driveway, rubbed his fingerprints off the wheel by habit, and got out. He let himself into the house, frowned at the telephone. He got a beer and a sandwich and went into the den where he sat down to keep vigil. A bit of a risk? Maybe. Maybe not. At least O'Shea was well hidden.

Wednesday night.

The O'Shea house was dark. The little girl slept sweetly with her nose snubbed into the plush hide of a toy animal. Mrs. King slept. Vee, on the couch in the living room, curled up, uncurled, turned over.

Anabel wasn't beautiful. She wasn't *anything* like Celia, thank goodness. Anabel listened. She even went and did things, on the basis of what Vee told her. It was a little frightening. It made Vee feel real. So she was trying not to dream, not to comfort herself with a dream about Beau Carlson, for instance, who had been very nice to her. But it did not mean anything and she must not pretend that it did. Must not pretend at all? That was very hard.

But Anabel wasn't like Lillian, either. Not "sweet." Not thinking about how "sweet" her manners ought to be or whether she was acting like a lady. The thing about Anabel, she was real. And Vee had seen the vision, but she wasn't sure that she herself could bear it. Vee didn't know what she really was. She had always been trying so hard to be, or to dream that she was, something else.

Anabel was loyal. But she said what she thought, too. Vee did not know whether to be loyal still, or what? Or what? There were some things Anabel didn't understand. Some things she had not believed. Vee couldn't blame her, but she wished . . . But if Anabel ever did understand those things . . . !

Vee curled, uncurled. . . .

Anabel was trying to lie quietly in the big bed, all alone, and not give the terrible shadow of the hitchhiker any more substance than it deserved. But logic ran. If the man in the raincoat had been Pat, Pat would have called her. He had not. Therefore, he wasn't Pat. If he wasn't Pat, then he had taken Pat's raincoat. If he had taken Pat's raincoat, how had he done that?

No, no, wait. The premises were only probable. All right, she knew about probability. She knew that, however great, it still remained only probability.

Could she dream up any other premises? What if Pat had been hurt, say, going off the road in the car? Had been thrown out, or had jumped out and got up to the road? Had been dazed? Hadn't been able to think who he was, who she was? Had been the man in the raincoat after all?

It's possible, she whispered in the dark.

Wednesday night.

Carlson sat on a hard chair in the hospital corridor, outside Mrs. Adams' door. There was a certain fluttering around the nurses' station. Women-in-white tripped past him rather more often than was absolutely necessary. Miss More was haughtily quiet, trying to forget how she had fallen apart under those cool young eyes. Well, the man on the phone had sounded *hysterical!* How could she have let his call go through to a patient? She *had* told him that his wife was doing very well, nothing to worry about. She *had* done her duty. Her full duty. She was forty years old and she'd been doing her duty a long, long time and that young man needn't have been so insolent. Not that he had said anything. He had been insolent, just the same.

Miss More "humphed" to herself, remembering how they had moved Celia Adams' roommate, how Celia had played possum. Oh, she hadn't been asleep! Oh no—lying there, so pretty! Mrs. Adams had seen the young man peering in at her. And the green eyes opening, and that long cold stare between them. The insolence of young good-looking people who recognized their kind. Miss More settled her starched feathers. None of *her* business.

Carlson shifted his rump on the hard chair. Nobody had showed. He'd had a bit of a shock. If it hadn't been for the uncanny resemblance to Cecil Wahl, he would have picked the old biddy in the maroon thing to have been the Adams woman.

Thursday

ANABEL must have been asleep; something had wakened her. The sound of weeping. Someone was weeping in her house. In the night? In the first faint dawn. It wasn't the child.

It isn't I, is it? wondered Anabel.

After a minute, she put her feet out of the bed, felt for her slippers, and groped for her robe. She turned on no lamp; she knew where the furniture was. It was Vee Adams, of course, weeping on the couch in the living room, and Anabel felt impatient with her, for the sound of her distress that was so distressing. She went into the living room, made her way to the couch, and sat down on the edge of it, saying nothing.

"I'm sorry. I'm sorry. I'm sorry." The girl lashed herself.

Still Anabel did not speak, but silently, now, she gave the girl permission to weep. Very well, then, weep. In a world that is too much for you. Poor kid, you cannot cope, and so you weep. So do we all.

Vee said, "I think about myself too much. I know I do. But my mother is dead. And my father isn't my father anymore. Or anything like my father used to be. Celia doesn't see me. There's nobody to think about me, except me. I know. I know. Probably I am jealous. But even when I leave myself out of it, there is still something wrong with her.

"You don't know, Anabel. It was wrong, a long time ago, and it gets wronger and wronger. It isn't only that she steals. She doesn't do *anything* like other people. And you can't love her. I mean, if you do, she doesn't give anything back. I know because I did love her, at first. And my father still doesn't care for anything else on earth but Celia. She doesn't care for him one bit. She only . . . But I don't hate her, either. You can't even hate her. You can't do *anything* with her. There's something wrong."

"*Ssh* . . ."

"I'm sorry. I'm sorry. I don't know what's right to do. For me to do, I mean."

"It wouldn't be right," said Anabel softly, "to wake my mother."

"I know. I know. Were you asleep?"

Anabel put her hand on the girl's shoulder where she could feel the vibrations of distress. She was wide awake now, and she began to think that she had made a hasty judgment, fitting this individual into a familiar pattern, the stepchild, the beautiful young stepmother, and . . . oh sure . . . the "inevitable" reaction of jealousy.

So Anabel said, very softly, "But I'm listening, now."

Vee turned over. "Sometimes I think she wasn't all-the-way born. I know that sounds crazy. But she's not alive, except when her brother comes and then . . ." The girl's whole body shuddered. "Sometimes I think they didn't get split evenly. She hasn't got her whole half."

Anabel's brain said "fraternal twins," but she did not voice a correction. She listened.

"She's been killing my father for a long time," Vee said quite soberly.

"Oh, Vee . . ."

"Yes. Listen. She went to the college and stole a very expensive thing out of the lab. And when my father found out, he covered up for her. If it had been me . . . Oh, Anabel, my father and my mother would have marched me right up . . . But my mother died."

"Celia? Stole?" said Anabel. "But now wait . . . Pat told me about that. About some boy."

"Yes. Jim Rossi."

"But, Vee, if you knew . . ."

"Yes, that's it," said Vee. "So now, you see? It makes me think that I could have stopped it. If my father is doing terrible things, it's because she's made him. If I had told somebody *then,* maybe . . . I mean, if anybody had known what she was like and what he was getting to be like. I was either being loyal or else . . . just chicken. But I never was one of the lucky ones. Anabel, I don't know how to do things like that. Nobody ever listens to me. Except *you.*"

"*Ssh* . . ."

Anabel was bewildered. She was getting the sense of the girl's conviction that her father had been progressively corrupted. A jealous delusion? Very probably. Yet, *stealing!*

"How could your father cover up stealing?" she demanded.

"He took it back," said Vee. "Or one just like it. It came in the mail, on Monday morning. I . . . knew."

"Took it back? To the Provost, maybe?"

"He was going to sneak it back."

"Sneak? And just let that boy—?"

"He was so upset, Dad was. It was just about killing him. Just killing him, Anabel. But he was going to do it, just the same. For her. I mean, do you see?"

Anabel said, "Pat must have found that out."

The girl sighed herself deep into the couch cushions. "Yes," she said.

"He would have been furious."

"Yes."

Anabel gnawed her lips in the dark. All right. This explained what Vee had seen in the parking lot. Pat, angry, pursuing Everett Adams to thrash it out, and Everett fleeing. But it explained only that and no more.

"But what could have happened, then?" murmured Anabel.

"If I had only gone and told . . . If I had only gone and told . . . Then my father couldn't have tried to save her. And nothing would have happened to Mr. O'Shea." Vee turned over again, face down.

Now, in Anabel's mind, the pattern turned over, end-for-end, and she understood what Vee was thinking. It was true that, since Everett Adams' phone call to Mrs. Newcomb, no one could any longer imagine that Pat had sent him over the brink in the Rambler to his death, or to hide it. He was not dead. But Vee had been thinking of it the other way around. His own daughter seemed to be able to imagine that Everett Adams could have killed and run, that he could have become so lost a soul. In a brown rain-coat.

"No, no," said Anabel aloud. She was thinking, Because of a theft? What was that? Kleptomania? Why on earth should Celia Adams steal anything unless she had an illness? But that could be understood. That could be treated. Everett Adams would be upset, yes. But not as upset as this, surely.

"What would you do?" Vee whispered. "Would you go to the police and tell them, now?"

"Would I? Yes, I probably would. I'd certainly tell the Provost. That doesn't mean I'm telling you . . ." Anabel lost track of what she was saying. She was tired, very tired, and sick at heart.

"It's too late now," burst Vee. "*I* can't do anything about it. I'm sorry. I'm sorry. But *I* don't mean anything. I never will."

"Try not to feel so . . ." Then Anabel O'Shea pulled herself up. All right. Here is this girl. I didn't like her. I didn't want her. I didn't ask for her to be around. But here she is. So Anabel said, quietly, "Try not to be so stupid. Your mother died. Your father's left you, in a way—or so you say. But you didn't die. If your heart goes on beating, you had better mean something."

The girl was very still. Anabel could feel how Vee's heart was beating. She could feel her own. "Look at what you are saying," she went on. "Your father fell in love with Celia, who has got something wrong with her. He's let that make him do, you say, terrible things. But we don't know whether there's been a terrible crime. And if there has been, we don't know who has done it. And I'll tell you this. If Pat has done it . . . and somebody proves that to me . . . I'll still love him. But it's not going to make me be a criminal. Other people can make you very unhappy. But *they* can't make you meaningless."

She touched the girl's hair. "Think about what to do, in the morning. There's not much left of this night anyhow. All right?"

Vee said, very calmly and thinly, in the dimness, "I could never come and live with you."

Anabel said, "No."

"All right," said Vee. "Then I won't dream of it."

Anabel got up and made her way back to her bed, in her quiet house. She got in, shivering, and pulled up the blankets. Not much left of this night . . . so cold upon the mountain.

At a few minutes before eight in the morning, on Thursday, Cecil Wahl parked Mrs. Newcomb's car three blocks away from the hospital, where he had found a spot just behind a driveway so that he could get the car out, fast, if need be. He supposed that wherever he went, from here, it would be quickly. If Celia, and only Celia, knew (by now) where Ev was, then that was one thing. Otherwise, then otherwise. Cecil fancied himself the little pig who got up an hour earlier than the wolf.

But as he swung into the lobby, he almost collided with one of the wolves. "Morning, Mr. Wahl. I guess you've heard," said Maclaren.

"I hear from the neighbor that Ev phoned last night," said Cecil brightly. "Does anyone know where he is?" Cecil was tethered to the floor by the merest thread. If Ev had turned himself in somewhere, then Cecil was turning around and getting out, right now. But he read on the other face that this was not so. "Has he phoned my sister?" Cecil inquired.

"He hasn't talked to her. They told him, last night, that he could speak to her by nine A.M. Carlson's upstairs, been waiting on him. After you?"

Cecil preceded him into the elevator. He didn't like the sound of things. He might have one hour's margin left.

Maclaren pushed the button for the fourth floor. "What business are you in, Mr. Wahl?"

"What? Oh, excuse me. Sales." Cecil looked vague.

"I see. This development changes the picture a little bit. At least, we know that Adams is alive somewhere."

"May have nothing to do with O'Shea," said Cecil, nodding wisely.

"That's right. But the Service Detail got a fingerprint off the Rambler. Did you know?"

Cecil's head went high, his ears seemed to cock.

"Back of the mirror, as usual," Maclaren went on. "Somebody readjusted it. Well, sir, they lifted the prints and one thing . . . they aren't O'Shea's."

"Is that so?" drawled Cecil.

"We haven't gotten hold of Adams' prints yet. We don't have everybody's . . . handy." Maclaren smiled at his own pun.

Cecil did not smile. He looked as if he might whistle. The elevator stopped. Cecil had his hands in his pockets, his mouth pursed to whistle, his eyes staring at nothing. Maclaren reached out and opened the door.

Cecil went springily down the corridor. Maclaren seemed to amble after him. Carlson got off his chair to greet them. Cecil gave Carlson one quick nervous nod and

hurried into the room where Celia was. A nurse came fluttering to protest, but Maclaren stopped her. Then the two
policemen stepped silently into the room.

The two faces, so alike. The two very blond heads, almost white. The two pairs of green eyes. It was like watching somebody look at himself in a mirror.

Cecil murmured, "Poor C. I won't stay, now. Only be
in the way. Good luck to us all, eh?"

Celia said, "Poor Ev. He's such a fool, C. Maybe he
won't call."

Cecil said, "Maybe not. Even so. Another hour—? Shall
I call you, C?"

She closed her eyes. One source of green flame went out.
Cecil looked around, saluted with a lift of his hand and a
nod of his head and sprang away.

But the words between them hadn't told the half of it;
not the half of what had been said. Maclaren muttered
something, raced down the corridor, and got into the elevator with Cecil again. Cecil eyed him sideways and said
nothing.

Maclaren said, "She's right. Maybe he won't call. The
thing is, if he sent O'Shea's Rambler off that road, then
we can be pretty sure he knows where O'Shea may be. Will
you be at the Adams house later on? If we can get Adams'
prints there for comparison, that would be helpful."

Cecil said sweetly, "Naturally, I want to be as helpful
as possible."

"Then could you let me have a key to the house?"

"No key. Sorry. But the back door won't lock. Be my
guest." Cecil had his hands in his pockets. His head was
bent. He seemed ready to sprint off his mark. Maclaren was
the one who opened the elevator door.

Maclaren watched him go. He watched him through the revolving door. Then, Maclaren went over to the switchboard, to wait there.

Upstairs, Carlson sat down in the comfortable chair beside Celia's bed. There was no phone in the room yet. When a call came for her the nurse, following the normal procedure, would bring one and plug it in. Nothing to do but wait. Carlson said so, out loud.

The beauty on the bed rolled her fair head and said, "Who are you, pray tell?"

But she didn't care.

The old woman had actually bathed him. She seemed to realize, now, that he was seriously ill. She seemed to have been hearing echoes of his cries for cleanliness. So she had bathed him, and dusted him lavishly with talcum powder as if he were her infant, muttering all the while her private affirmations and incantations. No fear. No fear. He'd see. He'd see.

Pat saw, well enough, that he was in a bad way. He did not know what was happening to his leg, except that it was nothing good. The head he didn't worry about. But the arm, his right arm, had swollen all the way to the shoulder. His heart, he thought, was fighting the good fight. He seemed to be able to detach and observe the civil war within, the poison attacking, and his body's defenses.

Time would tell. Time would tell. But he didn't think it would take much longer for time to tell.

The old woman was wringing out her rag over the bowl on the table. Pat put his left forefinger into the thick coating of white talcum that lay upon the sheet. Almost whimsically, he lifted it and began to write upon the back of her black dress.

She felt his touch and turned.

"Ma?" he murmured. It was the magic word. He knew he was almost smiling, a sickly smile.

"I'll take care," she said. "No fear. You'll see." She turned back to her task and Pat wrote upon her back the big letters S O S. She seemed pleased that he had touched her. She turned again and beamed upon him. As she carried the bowl away toward the kitchen, Pat saw with squinted eyes that he had got the S's backwards, like a child's printing. Oh well. . . .

In a little while, he would get up and walk away from here.

In another little while . . .

He lay and breathed in the perfume from the talcum. It was a small keen pleasure.

Celia said, "Why should you eat three meals a day? Why not six? Five? Four? One? Why should you sleep eight hours? Suppose you don't feel like it? Why should you wear a skirt? A shoe? Why should you wash your teeth or pay money? Or work at some stupid job? Why should you do what everybody else does? Get married? Say 'please' and 'thank you'? Why is that?"

Carlson felt his Adam's apple moving. He had no answer. Her face was pale and her green eyes expressed an inner state to which he had no clue at all.

"Stupid," she said. "When nobody lives forever, why won't they let you live while you're at it? Why do you always have to do what they say? Who says?" Her head rolled.

"Shall I call a nurse?" He was reduced to conventional concern.

"Even when you're sick they still tell you what to do. Who gave them the right to tell you what to do? What *not* to do? Why is it?" cried Celia out of some anguish he couldn't understand. "Why is it they won't let you be with the only one—? Who are they to say? Who *are* they?" She raised herself up. "Who makes all these rules, anyway? For this game? I'd just as soon not play anymore." Her green eyes met his eyes. "And you," she said, "can . . ." She told him, in language that raised his eyebrows, what he could do. But she didn't care what he did.

A nurse stood in the door. "Telephone for Mrs. Adams. It's early, but the man downstairs said to let it through."

"Let it through," said Carlson.

As soon as the phone had been plugged in, Carlson was right up beside her on the bed. He knew now that she was some kind of kook, and he wasn't going to trust her for one minute. His hand was on the shank of the phone with hers, forcing the instrument to stay an inch away from her ear. His cheek was on her pale hair. She didn't care. She said, wearily, indifferently, "Hello?"

"Oh, my darling, are you all right?"

"Everett?" Her voice was flat.

"Mrs. Newcomb said you were fine. I tried to call . . . Are you all right, really? Truly?"

"I'm fine," she said languidly. "How are—?"

"I understood, then, that you wouldn't be coming. Darling, I only wanted to tell you to bring some money. But that's no matter. You would have come to me if you could. That made me happy. But now we've had our answer. You are to live. I am to die. Because I am the guilty one. I killed O'Shea. Killed him."

Carlson's hand jerked in shock. He let the phone go, grabbed wildly at a lipstick that was lying on the table, snatched up a magazine, wrote on a gray inside page WHERE IS HE? There was a killer at the other end—a shy bird, then.

"But you are not guilty, my darling," continued Everett's ranting voice, "I want you to live and be happy. Oh, Celia, let me have something from this ruin? Celia, promise."

"I promise," she said passively, even stupidly. "Are you coming home now?" Carlson began to shake the magazine before her eyes.

"Going to my long home, darling. Long home. You must understand. Tell my poor Violet to try to grow up and be happy and forgive and forget me. Tell Mrs. O'Shea there is nothing . . . nothing to say."

Celia stared at the big red words that Carlson had written and read them, numbly, aloud: "Where is he?"

"O'Shea? Why, at the dump. Didn't I tell you? I left him . . . left him. And not found yet? Well . . . Well . . ." His voice was falling, note by note, on the scale. "I can't talk. This was only to say 'good-bye.' My darling. My lovely girl."

Carlson, with his teeth clenched, was scribbling on another page, WHERE ARE YOU?

"I'm at the desk," said Everett, as if he could see the words. "The woman's gone, for a minute. I knew they kept a gun ready—in case of trouble. I'll be sorry to trouble them. I was happy here."

Carlson was holding his new message and glaring fiercely, but Celia's green eyes looked into his eyes, not at the writing. He had a strange idea that there wasn't anybody there, behind the green.

"I shall look up at the mountain I named for you one night—remember?" Everett was raving. "Then, to die. It's nothing. I don't mind. I truly do not mind."

Carlson's fingers were bruising her shoulder. Celia winced and said at last, "Where are you?"

"Why, at Bedelia's, darling. Where I loved you. Where I do love you. I called to say. But I must go. I can't even pay for this, darling. Will you? I have no time. She'll be back. So the rest is—"

Carlson wrenched the phone to himself and shouted, "Adams? Where are you? Adams?"

"Cecil?" The voice was shocked.

"This is the police."

"Ah . . . Celia . . ." It was a long wail for the great sorrow of a final betrayal. Then Everett said, with quaint dignity, "I owe a cock to Asclepius. . . ." The phone went dead.

Carlson was looking grim. "They were tracing it," he said to the woman, "so you may as well tell me. Where is he? Where's this Bedelia's?"

"It's just a motel," she said lazily, "outside of Las Vegas."

While Carlson was getting the telephone ear of Captain Murch himself, Celia walked her fingers on the spread where it lay across her body.

"Adams is talking suicide in a motel called Bedelia's, outside of Vegas," said Carlson, putting the emergency first. "He's got a gun."

Murch spoke aside. "O.K. We're on that," he said in a second. "Go ahead."

"He says he killed O'Shea and left the body at the dump."

"That's for the Uniformed Branch. They'll get on it."

"That's about it, sir."

"Paid off, eh?" said Murch, relaxing. "Why did he kill O'Shea?"

Carlson's crispness abandoned him. "He didn't say, sir."

Afterwards, he said to the woman on the bed, "Don't give up yet, Mrs. Adams. Las Vegas police officers will get there and they may be in time to stop him."

She said, sulkily, "Why should they? If he doesn't want to play anymore?"

"He's wanted for murder, for one thing," snapped Carlson, who was a cop.

She paid no attention. "Won't meet *him* again." She shuddered. "I don't believe that. This is all there is; there isn't any more. And who needs it? It's not so—great."

The young man stared. He stirred himself and went away.

Carlson got down to the lobby and looked around for Maclaren. He was standing by the switchboard with his ugly head bent as if he were praying. Carlson shook off a feeling of irritation. "You on the line?" he asked cheerfully.

Maclaren lifted his head. "Yes."

"Well, now we know, eh? I got it out of her where this motel is."

"I was on the line to Murch, too."

"They may get to Adams."

"They may. A gun's quick, though."

"Poor slob," said Carlson. "Well, maybe they won't. But even so, at least we know."

Maclaren said nothing but began to walk toward the exit.

"Headquarters?" chirped Carlson, keeping pace with. him.

"We'll have to go tell Mrs. O'Shea. And the little Adams girl."

"Yeah, that's right." Carlson's spirits were suddenly sent down. "Why the hell *would* Adams kill O'Shea?" he demanded almost indignantly.

"We don't know that," said Maclaren sadly.

"Cheese," said Carlson to his private section of the revolving door. "Does a cop have to know everything?"

When they got to the car, Maclaren took the driver's seat. Carlson sat beside him, pulling at his own fingers. They were almost to Pine Street when Carlson spoke at last. "Oh boy," he said, "that Adams dame—she's a bird. I'm telling you. She couldn't care less."

Maclaren shot a glance at him.

"What did you think," said the young man, "of her and her brother? Kind of weird. Right?"

"Brother has taken off."

"What do you mean?"

"Oh, he's gone. And she knows it."

"What's the matter with *him?*" (Carlson felt this to be true. Maclaren was right.)

"Something."

Carlson sucked air through his teeth. "Yeah," he said, "something. Maybe I see what you mean. Those two. I guess there's a lot of strange things. She gave me the shakes, practically."

"How was that?"

"Oh— Why should you do like everybody else? Why should you join the human race? That's what she was saying. She wants to know who makes the rules. She doesn't want to play anymore, she says. And I'll tell you another thing." Carlson cleared his throat. "She's got no religion. 'I won't meet him again,' she says, 'and who needs it? Life's not so great.'"

Maclaren was braking the car. He waited for an opening and made a U-turn.

"What's up, Dad?" said Carlson, a little too brightly because he could guess.

"We've got rules," said Maclaren grimly. "Being cops, we're not supposed to let it happen."

They raced back to the hospital, where they came too late.

Anabel was talking to the Provost on the telephone. She'd reached him at home; it was not quite twenty minutes after eight, in the morning. "Vee Adams and I agree that you ought to know. Celia Adams stole that objective (wasn't it?) from the lab. Everett Adams knew it, covered up, and was going to sneak it back. So at least you can put that student, whatever-his-name-is, out of his misery."

"My dear Mrs. O'Shea!" Anabel's style was too fast for Mr. Drinkwater. He was almost panting. "I do wish that Adams had come to me. I would have done everything in my power, I assure you . . ."

Anabel had no time for his regrets or his assurances. She excused herself. She wanted the line open for news. From the hospital, she said. (From the mountainside.)

She nodded at Vee, who smiled and went down on the carpet to join Sue and the doll family. Vee wasn't going to her classes. She had announced that she intended to go to see Celia, later today. She looked very tired, yet better somehow.

Anabel could see her mother out on the porch rummaging in the mailbox. She fingered the morning paper where, over a short article on the front page, the headline said PROF'S CAR WRECK IN PASS.

"The whereabouts of popular young instructor, Elihu (Pat) O'Shea. . . "

The whereabouts. Whereabouts. The word fell out of all its associations, a freakish collection of sounds. Anabel shook herself and wondered whether to call anybody and ask for news or whether to wait. And whether she could wait. It was the waiting, the waiting, the not-knowing-yet, the waiting, that ground one down. Her mother came in with a package in her hands which she was turning over and over. "Anabel, what's this?"

Anabel took it, a manila envelope fat with some content not its size. It was addressed to Pat, but Anabel tore off one end without hesitating. The thing inside was Pat's wallet. There was no money in it, but all his credit cards, his pictures. One of herself simpered up at her. Anabel couldn't believe her eyes. She peered again at the envelope and the postmark.

Then her heart went heavy because there was only one explanation that she could think of, and it was very probably the right one. She went back to the telephone and dialed the police. Neither Maclaren nor Carlson was there, so Anabel demanded, and got, Captain Murch. "Mr. O'Shea's wallet just came in the mail," she told him, speaking low. (The game on the carpet was going well.) "I've heard that when a thief strips a wallet and throws it away, anyone who finds it can put it in a mailbox and the post office will return it to the owner. Is that true?"

"I believe, in some communities . . ."

"It was mailed in Barstow." (There *was* a thief. And if a thief, was there a hitchhiker?)

"I see. Thank you, Mrs. O'Shea." His voice changed. He was gathering himself. "I'm sorry to have to tell you some news that is not very happy for you. You are not alone, are you?"

Now everything fell down about her, her heart, her tensions. She felt all heavy and flabby, a lump, with arms and legs.

"No. Go on."

"Adams phoned the hospital at 8:06. Carlson was on the line. Adams says . . ."

"Go on." The lump could speak. It was alone, of course. In the universe, it was all alone.

". . . that he left your husband's body at the dump. He says he killed him. Adams now . . ."

She kept on listening, politely, because this was confusing. It was probably true, but impossible, of course.

". . . says he is going to do away with himself." The captain cleared his throat. "In a fit of remorse. We have alerted the police in Las Vegas. They may get to him, but frankly, it is not likely. Adams has a gun."

Both of them dead, then? thought Anabel. "*Where* did you say?" (Pat's child was not twenty feet away, playing with the dolls. And the other man's child.)

"At a place called Bedelia's, a motel—" the captain began.

"No, no. Where he left—?"

"Oh—the dump. We have men on their way to the city

dump, Mrs. O'Shea. I am very sorry. We don't know how or why it happened. This is really all we know, so far."

"Yes."

It's enough, she thought. She put the phone down. The whole world was colorless. Her little golden daughter, on the sea-green rug, played in black and gray. "Anabel?" said Mrs. King.

Anabel got up and walked very fast into her own bedroom. Her mother followed her.

"Mother," said Anabel, having told her, "there is only one thing you can do for me. Be with Sue. Take that off me. I've got to get out of here until I can bear it. Until the time comes to tell her, or bear to wait and not tell her. Mother, you are the only one in the world who can do that for me. A little while? A little minute?"

"Of course I will, Anabel. But shouldn't you lie down? Take something?"

"No, no. I'll walk," said Anabel. "Just walk. It has to sink in. What's the use of making that take longer? One thing, though, before I can go. I'll have to tell Vee. Oh, what shall we do with her, Mother? How can I leave her on you too?"

Mrs. King said, "You do what you must do, Anabel. So will I. And so will she. And so will Susie too—when the time comes. I'll send Vee in here."

Anabel looked at herself in the glass. You are going to be a widow, she said to herself. A very young widow. Very soon. Just as soon as your whole soul can stop screaming that it can't happen to you. It can happen.

When Vee came in, Anabel said quietly, "I can't do anything for you, Vee. So I'll just tell you what was said to me." She repeated the words of Captain Murch exactly as they were burned, forever, into her brain. "Adams has a gun," she finished.

Vee had put her palms to her temples and pulled back the flesh of her face. She looked like a cat. "I was afraid. I was afraid."

"Hang on now," said Anabel sharply.

"I'm sorry."

"We're all sorry."

"My father . . . must have been sorry—?"

"Yes, he was sorry. Vee, I've got to go. Stay in here if you want to."

Vee said, "But oh, Anabel, we were so close. So close."

"What?" Anabel was, of all things on earth, powdering her nose. She would get out of here in a minute. She was only waiting for the girl to collapse. Or not, as the case would be. Or maybe Anabel wouldn't get out of here. She might have to just . . . rock with it, right now.

"Yesterday," Vee said, "we were so close. We were even *on* Oleander Street."

"What are you talking about?"

"But that's . . . where, isn't it? I told you, there's a dumping place. Didn't you say a dump?"

"Yes."

"But that's where, then. It was on their way."

Anabel was astonished that her brain could receive and function. "We never did say anything to the police about the gas station, the boy . . . the way Pat went. The *city* dump's the other side of town!"

"I know. That's what I mean. This place is way out at the very end, where Dad used to . . ."

Anabel knew what she was going to do. She didn't ask it to be wise or sensible. She didn't query it at all.

She said to Vee fiercely, "You've got to take a thing like this right in your teeth. *You've* got to live. I told you. Will you do something for me?"

Vee staggered and said, "Yes. I will, Anabel." She took her hands from her head. They trembled.

"Call the police. Get Captain Murch. You can do it," Anabel insisted, as Vee quailed. "You're the one who *can* do it. Tell him about this dump, at the end of Oleander. They are going to the wrong place. Tell him. Just that. That's all."

"I . . ."

"It's something for you to do."

"All right. Where are you going?"

"I am going where Pat is," said Anabel, without taking any thought at all, "because if I don't, I will never, to the end of my life, forget that I didn't."

Carlson gazed upon the smashed thing on the sidewalk as coolly as became a man and a cop. Then he swallowed the sour spittle in his mouth and looked around for what needed doing. Maclaren was talking to an intern. Celia had jumped almost as soon as they had driven off. There had already been photography, questions and answers. The ambulance stood ready. Celia was for the morgue.

Carlson spotted a wretched lad almost prostrate on the curb, still being sick enough to constitute a public nuisance, so he strode over to pick him up. He put the sufferer up on a low stone wall and asked whether a doctor was needed. "What's your name?" Carlson would not have been surprised to see the boy lose consciousness.

"Name's Parsons. Mike Parsons. I never saw anything like that. I never want . . ."

"All right. All right." Carlson waved away a gathering audience.

"I was actually trying to get in and find out . . . about her. Then I saw her jump. Why did she do it?" The green face turned up. (Parsons could not imagine. Parsons had snooped once too often.) "Terrible," he whimpered.

"Take it easy," said Carlson. "You wanted to find out *what* about Mrs. Adams?"

"Well, see, it's so kinda funny. They say . . . around school, I mean . . . maybe she didn't really have an operation. Maybe there was something going on . . . Her and O'Shea."

Carlson fixed him with a cold glare. "I'll tell you something, sonny," he said. "You're never going to find out anything, the way you're going."

"Hey, look! She better not . . ."

Carlson looked. A car had stopped across the street on the rim of the gathered people. Vee Adams was getting out of it. So Carlson went pushing through, as fast as he could go, and put himself in front of her. "No," he said. "I won't let you."

"I had to come." She was already shuddering, in great waves.

"Well, you're going back again."

"It is Celia?"

Maclaren was there, suddenly. "There's no question of identity," he said in his sad way. "This isn't necessary, Miss Adams. Who called you?"

"The Provost. He'd been called. He knew I was at Anabel's. I tried to reach Celia's brother, but he doesn't answer. So I . . . My dad would have wanted her to have somebody of her own. Maybe that's silly . . . But *I* have to live. . . ."

Carlson almost knew what she was talking about. Maclaren seemed to understand perfectly. "Stand aside, Jimmy. It's not too bad. She can take it."

So Vee looked between the standing people, then over their heads as the stretcher went up into the waiting vehicle. Just a red-and-white sheet over something flat.

Carlson grabbed her. "All right. Now you had better go home. Will that man take you?"

"Mr. Dickenson? I don't know. He lives next door to Anabel's house. He was very nice . . ."

"*We* have to see Mrs. O'Shea," said Carlson. "Listen, we can take you." He signaled to the frightened-looking face in the car and the car moved away. Carlson led her to their car and put her into it. He told her what would be done now with what was left of Celia.

She was shivering. He didn't know how to tell her any more. Then he realized that he need not. Vee said, "It seems as if everybody's dead. Mr. O'Shea. My dad. And Celia. It's . . . awfully strange."

Carlson got in at her right and put his arm behind her. "Oh, look, Violet—I mean Vee—I'm sorry."

"We are all sorry."

"But I mean, because I goofed this one. I don't know what to say to you. I should have figured what she had in mind. I just goofed, that's all. If I had only . . . If I'd had any sense," he said bitterly. "I just didn't take it in. It didn't get to me. I didn't know her really, but that's the more reason I should have listened."

Vee said, "I guess you can't be sure you could have made any difference."

He looked at her intently. Listening.

Maclaren was standing at the other side of the car now. "Mrs. O'Shea is at home, is she?"

"Oh no, Anabel's gone to the end of Oleander Street. Because that's where Mr. O'Shea must be. And she . . . Well, she *would* go. I mean, if you knew her . . ."

"Where?" said Maclaren. They both had their heads turned to her now and seemed to be listening, very intently. So Vee managed to tell them about the old dumping place, the gas station boy, the reasons to believe.

Maclaren had heard of the place. "Out by Mrs. Pryde's," he said. "Old Mrs. Pryde lives way out there—that's if she's still alive. I guess you wouldn't know about her and her son. Johnny Pryde. That was before your time."

Carlson said impatiently, "Does anybody else know about this? Does the department?"

"I told them," said Vee. "I said I would." And then she lifted both her hands, "Did I? Oh yes, I did! A long time before the Provost called. I *think* I did. I *promised*."

"Don't worry," said Carlson, watching her. "We can check." He opened the glove compartment and took out the phone that was hidden there. He spoke into it. Finally, he said, "We'll get out there, right away. *I'd* say Miss Adams knows what she's talking about."

He put the phone away and said, "Yes, you told them. But they've got men out taking a good look at the city dump and they're being thorough. We better. . . ." Then Carlson, ignoring his partner's claim to be familiar with the end of Oleander, let his left arm come down around Vee's shoulders. "You can show us how to get there, Violet? I mean, Vee?"

"Violet's all right," she said dully. "Yes, I'd be glad if I could do something."

Carlson looked over her head at Maclaren, rather defiantly. Maclaren nodded and started the car.

Stan Simmons, who lived on Oleander Street, took the truck home with him nights. This was permitted because Mr. Johanneson and Stan's father were old friends and there was an unwritten covenant that Stan was not only apprentice but also heir to the grocery store. Stan's future was clear before him and he was content with it. He had the temperament for a neighborhood business. So, of course, Stan would not skylark in the truck on his own time. And it was convenient.

As he came along Oleander Street on Thursday morning, Jamie Montero was already on his perch by the gate, waving at him to stop. Mary Montero was out there too.

"Stan! Stan!"

"Hi, ma'am. Jamie? I got something for you." Stan tossed the gift.

Jamie caught it. "Take me out to the witch's, Stan?"

"Well, gee, I suppose so." Stan, once in a while, had taken the little cripple on his rounds, although never without permission from his mother and from Mr. Johanneson. "I'll be going out there this afternoon. O.K.?"

"No, now. Right now!"

"Gee, listen. I'm supposed to—"

"Something's funny. There's a Ford."

"Yeah? Thought it was a Chevy." Stan winked at Mrs. Montero.

"No, no. This Ford came by last night, real late, and it

went away but now it's back. He's looking for the bad man."

But Mrs. Montero said, in a nervous way, "If you could take five minutes . . . Honest, Stan, I don't see how else he's going to get any sleep at night. Maybe if he got out there once he'd stop all this. *I* can't get it out of his head. His father wants to whip him, but that's not going to get him to sleep either."

Stan looked at the wan little face. "Listen, Jamie, you don't want to make yourself sick, do you? You ought to forget it. I mean it."

"I wish I could walk," said Jamie passionately.

That did it, of course. Stan winced and looked at the mother's face and he said, "Hey, come to think of it, I do have a question to ask the old witch at that. Make a good enough excuse, I guess. So . . . O.K., Mrs. Montero?"

"Yes. I wish you would, Stan. But take care of him."

"Oh, don't you worry." Stan got out and lifted the boy into the truck. "You keep your window rolled up, mind. In case the dog is out. What's the matter with you anyway? Didn't I tell you there's nobody out there?"

"There's somebody out there now," said Jamie confidently.

Cecil Wahl was out there.

With a wary eye on the house where the dog lived, he was hunting for the flashlight. It belonged to Mrs. Newcomb. She would know it, say it traveled with her car, say who had had her car. Cecil had no intention of being quite that helpful to the police.

He was a slow and conservative driver (with his peculiar handicap) and it had taken him forty-five minutes from the hospital to the end of Oleander. But it wasn't quite nine o'clock yet. He could afford to hunt until he found the flashlight with his fingerprints on it.

Then he'd be gone. Once he got out of the cul-de-sac of Oleander Street, it would be simple.

Even when they picked up Ev—the man was such a fool, he'd stall around battling his "conscience," whatever that was—it would take them a while to get the whole story. Even after that, since Ev thought he was protecting Celia, they'd have to check *her* out. Dig up that old incident? Take time.

Celia could tell them all about it, of course. But he knew his sister. She wasn't really vindictive. She hadn't the energy for that. She might very well just give up, just not bother, just stare at the wall. (Until somebody like Everett Adams came along and knocked himself out to "save" her.)

All of this would give Cecil, who was interested in saving himself, plenty of time. The only question in his mind right now was whether to steal the Newcomb car. For all his bravado about a man on foot, it might be smart to take the car as far as L.A., say. Or south?

The whole silly affair was a nuisance to him. He didn't have much cash. He hated work, the kind of labor he'd have to do to eat. For a while. It was too bad that Ev, having got himself into this jam, was alive to tell the tale and start the police along the way that Cecil couldn't afford to have them go. Cecil would have found it rather relaxing to move into Everett's comfortable house, fake up a skin disease, perhaps, on his right hand. (He had done that before.) Just hang around, comfortably, until the estate was settled. That would have been quite an improvement over running.

But Cecil did not doubt that he could run successfully,

that he would eat. He had a superabundance of self-confidence, a kind of extra portion. It made him merry and quick and willing to take chances. But the only chance he saw now was that Everett might not break down under police inquiry and tell about that old affair. Cecil could lie low, and if this miracle were to come to pass, he could always reappear.

So he'd find the flashlight . . . except that he couldn't seem to find it. Well, if some kid had already picked it up, it was safe enough. At least the police would not be the ones to find it. And a kid would cherish such a treasure and soon blur off the signs of Cecil's handling. This place was like the end of the world, though. No kid-signs. He had better keep on looking around. There was still time.

When he saw the panel truck come around the last curve, he did not startle or run or hide. He stood there, a little way in among the trees.

Stan parked the truck ahead of the Ford. "Hi!" He recognized this man as the one who had been in the store yesterday.

"Hi, there." Cecil was casual.

"Anything I can do?" Stan was full of goodwill and curiosity.

Cecil strolled nearer. "Just wondering about this land. A playground, is it?"

"No, no. Kids don't play out here. They're too scared of the old lady lives in that house. They think she's a witch." Stan grinned. "She might be, at that. You looking for a playground?"

"No, no. Who owns this grove, do you happen to know?" Cecil was improvising.

"Can't say I do. Maybe Mrs. Pryde owns it. Wait a minute and I'll ask her." Stan hit his horn.

He debated whether to ask the man for the price of the milk and the cookies. But he dismissed this as being too small. The cookies, opened, had been unsalable. But they had disposed of the cookies, they could hardly . . .

Jamie said, "Mister? Are you looking for a blue Chevy Bel Air?"

"Am I what?" Cecil cocked an eyebrow.

Stan started to explain, but the dog was barking, the door of the bungalow had opened. The old woman came out upon the stoop, closing the door behind her against some opposition. She began to hobble down toward the broken gate and she was screeching, "You bring the medicine? You, boy?"

She was thin, with wild white hair. She wore a black dress that looked as if it had been on her frame for years. She had a staff in her hands. Her eyes were wild. "Witch" was the only word for her.

Jamie quivered a little. Stan said, in an easy friendly tone (to reassure the boy), "Hi, Mrs. Pryde. What's this? Did you say medicine?"

Cecil had taken two steps backward, as if to put himself in a spectator's position, but the old woman had seen him. "Who's that?" She glared.

"Just a man wants to know if you own the eucalyptus grove."

"Not me. Not me. It don't bother me. Where's my stuff, you, boy?"

"Oh, I didn't bring it yet," Stan said. "But listen, we couldn't read one of the items. Hey, I'll bet that was the medicine."

She glared at him.

"Listen, if we can't figure out what you want, Mrs. Pryde, we can't put it in your order. Let's see, now. P O S H E A. That's what it looked like. What kind of medicine is it?" She didn't answer. "You're not feeling so well, Mrs. Pryde?"

She *was* looking wilder than usual, as a matter of fact.

Jamie piped up, "Did you see a blue Chevy Bel Air—?"

He might as well have been speaking Greek. Mrs. Pryde lifted her staff and pointed it at the child. "You don't come around here!" she shrieked. "Johnny Pryde don't want to play with you!"

"Listen, listen," said Stan placatingly, "if you're sick, Mrs. Pryde, do you want me to get you a doctor?"

"None of them. None of them." Her roving eyes caught Cecil's fascinated stare and she suddenly looked sly. "A touch of the influenza," she muttered. "No fear."

"Gee, that's too bad." Stan was doing his best. Mr. Johanneson carried some drugs and Stan knew what they were. "How about aspirin, maybe? You want me to bring you some aspirin, Mrs. Pryde?"

"You bring my stuff. You bring the good meat and all."

"Sure. Sure. This afternoon. My regular time." She had become calmer. Stan went on with his duty. "But Mr. Johanneson wants me to tell you— Listen, he's going to send that big meat order *this* time. But it's pretty expensive, he says."

The old woman suddenly lifted her staff again and pointed it over the hood of the truck to where Cecil was rooted. "I know you! I know you! You're a liar! Don't you say Johnny Pryde done it."

The dog, in the house, was frantic to get out.

Stan, despairing of the conversation ever making sense, put the truck in reverse and began to back it around the Ford, watching his rear. Jamie was trying to pierce through the trees with long eye-beams, looking for the Chevy. It was Cecil who saw the old woman turn her back. There were some whitish marks on the rusty black of her dress. A crooked squiggle, a drunken O, a blur. She beetled back to the stoop.

So Cecil knew, with one thing and another, where Pat O'Shea was, now.

Then Stan was calling to him. "Hey, better watch out for the dog, mister. He's pretty vicious and the old lady's nuts. You can see that. So if you don't want to get bit, better watch it. Boy, she's *really* nutty today."

"I'll watch it," said Cecil.

"See, she had this son, this Johnny Pryde." Stan was feeling chatty. "Well, he got into all kinds of bad trouble and actually, they ran him through the gas chamber, a long time ago. But you just heard her, talking as if he was still alive? Oh boy . . . I wouldn't tangle with her if I was you."

"Thanks a lot." Cecil looked tiptoe, ready to fly. But he did not move.

Stan, perceiving that he wasn't interesting his audience, began to back the truck farther. He said to Jamie, "I got to go. O.K.?"

The little boy's face was pale, his eyes were bright. He said nothing.

Cecil, left standing at the end of the road, was thinking hard. O'Shea was alive. The crazy old woman had him in there. He must have been injured.

So Cecil's time was up. By now, Ev must be blubbering and blabbing somewhere, and the cops would be out here, very soon. When they got here, they'd find O'Shea, who could tell and would tell, and right away, whatever it was that *he* knew. So time was up. Cecil must get lost, fast. Never mind the flashlight. He turned his head and looked into the grove and saw a brightness twinkling on the ground.

Maybe Cecil was a little bit obsessed about fingerprints. Sometimes he suspected that this was so. But this was the one thing, the one chance he never took, if he could help it. Something to do with Mom? Maybe. But if that was Mrs. Newcomb's flashlight shining in there, he could not leave it.

"Hey, Stan," said Jamie in the truck, "there *is* another road, in the trees."

"Naw, there isn't. It doesn't go anywhere." Stan wasn't thinking about Jamie. He was wondering about that tow-headed fellow. He had to get Jamie back and get to work, he'd lost enough time.

"Hey, Stan, Johnny Pryde really is dead, isn't he?"

"Oh, sure. Long ago. Listen," Stan said. "You get your sleep, now, and stop worrying your folks. O.K.? You don't want to get sick, do you?"

"Sick people die," said Jamie intensely.

"That's right," said Stan. "They sure do. I mean, some-times."

"Johnny Pryde was a bad man. It was O.K. if he died."

Stan was not following; he was watching the road. He said, "Well, for Pete's sakes!" An Oldsmobile was coming

toward him along Oleander Street. And the woman in it
was the same one—Stan hit his brakes.

Anabel had been driving skillfully, alertly, and quite fast.
She had thought, at first, that she ought not to be on the
roads at all, but this was not so. Everything seemed clear
and sharp to all her senses.

The thing was, she could not wait anymore. She must
go, now, to the end of the waiting. Get there. She had
waited and waited too long already. A terrible sorrow kept
coming up in a wave, ready to catch her by the throat. But
it always subsided, it sank away. And she could see the
road, the roadside, the cars, the world going about its business; then what she was doing would seem absurd. Incred-
ible.

But she was moving. She was going right into it, toward
it, *for* it. To an end. And a sad beginning.

She turned into Oleander Street, and wondered whether
the police had somehow passed her by. Maybe they were
there . . . out there at the end, where the end was. It
didn't matter. She had to get there. Then she saw the panel
truck and she saw that it was stopping, and that the boy in
it was staring at her.

Oleander Street was narrow. Anabel slowed. She braked.
She stopped because, in some way, the boy in the truck
knew her and it was a meeting.

She said, "Can you tell me? Is there a dump of some
kind, out at the end of this street?"

The boy's long thin freckled nose seemed to twitch. He
said, "No, ma'am. Well, not exactly. Well, yeah . . . I
guess some folks do throw stuff over into the arroyo. Can

I—" he seemed to know her and be curious about her—"do anything?"

"I'm Anabel O'Shea," she began, mechanically. (She had done this all day yesterday.) "I am looking . . ." She stopped, because this was stalling, busy-work, bitterly unnecessary, now.

"You looking for the bad man?" It was a boy's voice. It rang out from the spot beside the driver of the panel truck. There was a little boy in there.

The driver said, "Aw, come on, Jamie."

"I am looking for my husband," Anabel said.

"Oh," said the truck driver. "Yeah. Well, *he's* out there. I just been talking to him."

She was stabbed by the shock. Her breath came in. Her rib cage came up high. The heart jumped. The blood raced.

"With Pat?" she cried out. "With Pat?"

"Well, I mean," said Stan, "with the fellow in the store yesterday."

"The . . . what?"

"The grocery store? You made a phone call? I mean, there was this man with you. And *he's* out there."

The uproar in Anabel's body began to sicken and turn sour. "Out there?" she said.

"Oh, well, listen. I mean out at the end of Oleander. I mean, he's out there. I was just out there. Talked to him."

"To Cecil Wahl?" Anabel's head was spinning. "Has he found Pat?"

"I don't know what you mean, ma'am."

"Pat. Pat O'Shea." The boy looked stupid. Didn't understand. Anabel's head felt thick itself. They stared at each other.

Then the little boy said, "I guess I got to tell. The old

witch has got him. The bad man." He sounded ready to cry.

The driver turned his head and said severely, "For Pete's sake, Jamie, skip it about the bad man, will you?" He turned and said to Anabel, "Don't pay any attention. He's got something in his head and it isn't so. He doesn't know what he's talking about."

Anabel did not know what either of them was talking about. The truck driver had given her a terrible shock. Her whole body still throbbed and quivered with it. She said, "Well, thank you." She started the car moving.

Stan started up the truck and stopped, abruptly, at Jamie's gate, hurried to pluck him from the seat and put him back on his perch. He brushed off Mrs. Montero's gratitude. He was going to be late. He hurried along the rest of Oleander Street. That woman had looked awful wild or sick or something. Stan was feeling uneasy. He should have warned her about the dog. Well, but that tow-headed fellow was out there still. And Stan guessed he wasn't her husband after all, but at least they knew each other. Stan had warned *him*. So he guessed it was going to be all right. But it was certainly funny. What was this all about, anyhow? And where was that third person, he wondered, the girl who had been with these two in the store yesterday?

She was snug between Maclaren and Carlson. She was trying not to think about Celia, because she knew she would be thinking about Celia for a long long time. She didn't think about her father. She had let him go, a long long time ago. And he was gone. She didn't think about Mr. O'Shea. She tried to think about Anabel.

Although Maclaren drove fast, they seemed to be rushing through veils and cobwebs and many impediments. It was taking time. They were past the gas station where Dick Green worked, and getting out into the country, but there was a long way to go yet.

Vee said, "I'm afraid she's there already, all alone."

"We'll get there," Carlson said. He wasn't driving but his foot was on the floorboard, hard.

She breathed in deeply and sighed breath out. "It's all so . . ."

"Take it easy."

Vee looked at the rushing scenery. It wasn't easy. But it wasn't too hard, either. It was odd. To have them both dead, and find herself all alone, was not as lonely as it had been before. She said, quietly, in a moment, "Do you know, for sure, that my father is dead?"

Maclaren said, "Maybe we can check."

Carlson said, "Right." He got out the telephone. "Carlson. Any word from Vegas on Everett Adams?"

"Oh, there's word, all right," the voice said. "There's no such place."

"No such—?"

"No such motel. Captain Murch has had them trying Barstow. No soap there, either. And it's getting mighty late for this Adams. Somebody blew it."

Carlson choked. "Yeah. Thanks."

His smooth young face was blooming slowly red and redder. "Um, boy," he burst. "Dumb cop! That's me. Oh, listen, Violet. I'm sorry—I goofed that too. Your father . . . She lied to me, that's all. So there wasn't any chance for him."

"I don't understand, Beau, I mean, Mr. Carlson."

"Celia. *She* told me this motel—this Bedelia's—was around Vegas. But she didn't want him stopped. She didn't give a— She lied, and I fell for it, and God knows where he is."

"Take it easy," said Maclaren.

"Oh, sure," the lad said bitterly. He stared out his window. Maclaren drove steadily on.

"It isn't *named* Bedelia's," said Vee thoughtfully, in a minute. "I think the name of it is Sunset something-or-other."

"What?"

"Well, they had a long honeymoon. I was a camp counselor that summer. *They* always called it 'Bedelia's,' but I used to send postal cards and it was to Sunset-something. Courts, maybe."

"Do you know the address of this place?" asked Carlson quietly.

"I don't know the number. It's only up in Apple Valley."

Carlson's strong young hand trembled as he reached for the telephone.

After Carlson had sent the message, Maclaren said, "I ought to have asked you, Miss Violet. Didn't think to. Should have thought. There wasn't *much* chance for him, but there could have been more."

Vee said, "Celia killed him a long time ago, Mr. Maclaren. I mean, it isn't as if he was himself anymore. *My* father couldn't have done that terrible thing—to Mr. O'Shea I mean—if he was himself, the way he used to be. I don't want to sound—hateful. I don't hate her. I didn't ever hate her, as far as I know. But there was something wrong with her."

"With Celia?" said Carlson. "I guess *so*."

"It's awfully hard to explain, Beau. I mean, Mr. Carlson."

"Beau's all right," he said, "if it's easier."

When Anabel came to the end of Oleander Street, there, sure enough, was Cecil Wahl, standing beside a car. When he saw her he took a kind of quick step, almost a dance step. Or, he was something like a cat, twisting to land on its feet.

Anabel parked the Olds crookedly and tumbled out. She went pell-mell toward him. Toward the end.

"Where is he?" she cried.

Cecil grasped both her hands. "What's up? What's happened? What are you doing—?"

"He's dead. Everett Adams says so."

"Where is Ev?"

"He's dead too," wailed Anabel. "Did you find Pat? Please?"

"Now wait," said Cecil. His hands were so tight they hurt. "What is this about Ev? He is *dead*, you say?"

"He was going to shoot himself." Anabel fought to remember that other people had other concerns. "He called. He killed Pat. He left Pat . . . at a dump. But the police have gone to the wrong dump."

Cecil said, "Anabel, please. Ev is dead? Shot himself? What did you say?"

"They've told the Las Vegas police, but they don't think there's much chance—"

"Las Vegas?"

"Some *silly* name. Bedelia's . . . He had a gun."

"I see," drawled Cecil (who knew where Bedelia's was). "And the cops have gone to the wrong—dump, you say?"

"The wrong place," said Anabel. "There's a dump here somewhere. And Pat . . ."

She could feel that his hands had turned cold somehow. They began to release her. Cecil said, "There is a dump, Anabel. It's beyond those trees. Along that track."

"Have you . . . been?" Now she was not held and not leaning upon him in any way at all. She was leaning upon no one and nothing. Anabel was on her own feet. She said, sharply, "Will you tell me, please?"

"Look," he said, "why don't you sit in the car. I'll go . . . I'll get . . ."

"Is he there?" she demanded.

One of the man's eyebrows drew up. He cocked his pale head. His green eyes watched her. "Yes," he said, "he's down there."

He didn't look like a man who was telling bad news, reluctantly because he felt sorry. He looked like a man who was trying out a little jab, and watching to see the result.

Anabel felt a revulsion. She took two steps backward. She turned away from him. She started into the grove, along some ruts. She walked, then she began to skip along faster, in a half-stumble, half-run. Because this was the end of the road, the end of one world. She was almost there.

Cecil watched her go.

He'd seen a glimmer on his horizon. Ev was dead? The cops had gone to the wrong place? Twice over? They would not find Ev in time. They would not find O'Shea. Yet.

If Ev was dead, that left *only* O'Shea.

But Cecil knew where O'Shea was. And he was officially, you might say, already murdered. He was needing med-

icine, in the witch's house. Suppose he were to die in there?
It would be the same murder. For which the cops already
had the murderer's confession, and his suicide.

Safe as houses.

Cecil thought he could manage his sister.

Risky? But the stakes were so high. Why not? he
thought. When he had just been presented with what you
might call a free murder. Right here. If there was time for
it. If he could manage.

He had meant to divert Anabel and run. Well, she was
diverted. He could see her. She had sat down upon the
ground. Probably she was going to sit there and cry.

He could always say he'd been looking for a phone in
the witch's house. What about the dog, though?

Ah, now. When there is a gift—of time, of chance—
while the cops look in the wrong places, and Cecil was in
the right place and smart enough to see his chance, he must
be bold enough to take it!

Maybe around at the back of the house. There might be
a way that he could get at O'Shea. Because if he could . . .
if he could . . . and then phone Celia . . . Cecil was
home free!

He slipped between the two cars and put a tree between
him and the witch's house.

Anabel had come to the end. She was sitting on the brink
of the arroyo, gazing down at a rubbish heap upon which
had been thrown her husband's body. In a moment her
sick and frightened, straining eyes would see it. Cast off. A
piece of rubbish, like the rest. Then she would know, at
last, that Pat himself, that gay and loving man, was not
here at all. And not anywhere, in this world.

At the back of the bungalow there was a window with a busted screen. Cecil, hugging the wall, could hear the dog carrying on somewhere inside, and the old woman talking. Mad? She must be. Well, the point was, could he do it?

He crept to the window, which was rather high off the ground. His eyes came a foot above the sill, but he couldn't see in. There was a blind hanging crookedly.

Cecil said, "O'Shea?"

Within, a man's voice answered clearly, calmly. "That's more like it."

When Stan came into the store, Mr. Johanneson was leaning over the morning paper. "That was Mrs. O'Shea," he announced.

"I know," said Stan, astonished.

Johanneson glanced up at him. "I mean the woman who was in here yesterday."

"I know," said Stan again.

"You saw it in the paper? You figured it out too?"

"Huh?"

"Look here. Look here." The grocer rapped the paper with his knuckles. " 'PROF'S CAR WRECK IN PASS. The whereabouts of popular young instructor Elihu (Pat) O'Shea . . .' You didn't even hear her say she was going 'where Pat was.' How did you—?"

"Yeah, but she said 'Pat'—just now."

"Huh?" It was Johanneson's turn to be bewildered.

Stan leaned on the paper. "A Rambler? But how could he—?"

"How could he what? That was some rain last Monday night."

But Stan said, "Wait a minute. Wait a minute. You see

how they spell O'Shea, Mr. Johanneson? You see the initial?" Stan was hearing Jamie say, "The old witch has got
him."

The grocer looked at the paper. He looked up.

Stan said, "Gee, Mr. Johanneson, maybe we better call
the police, or something. Because Mrs. Pryde, she's *really*
nutty today."

"O'Shea?"

There was no sound in the landscape. The house held
sound, but not the land. The wild land baked, beyond the
back of the house.

"Present. Future. What? Who's that?" said the voice in
the house, closer than the dog's racket.

Cecil said, "I want to help you. But what about that
dog?"

"Eh, Rex?" The voice was jubilant. "Anabel sent you,"
it proclaimed.

"Yeah. Right. Do you think you could get over here?
To the back window?"

"Why, I might as well be over there as where I am."
Pat said, "Maybe better." His head was light. "I'll give it
the old try. If the good half of me can make it, stands to
reason the other half will go along. Wouldn't you say?
Friend? That's logical."

Pat slid his good left leg out of the bed. He struggled to
lift himself and turn, so as to get his right leg over and out,
but his right arm was such a big fat mess, he had no lever-
age.

". . . big fat mess," Pat muttered. "Now, I can't walk,
you understand. I absolutely cannot walk. On *two* legs, I

mean. That's out of the question. What is the question? *That* is the question."

Cecil waited.

Time passed.

Then Cecil's hands were through the window, batting the brittle, rustling blind aside. "Just close enough," he coaxed, "so that I can help you out. I've got a car. I'll get you to the car." (He would prefer to get this over with, right here. And then go virtuously around to the front door.) "I'm scared of the dog," he said.

"You're so right, friend," came the voice. "No you're not, either. Ought to be scared of the old woman."

"I am. I am," snapped Cecil. "Can you make it, O'Shea?"

"Why, I certainly can. Very happy to meet you. Halfway. Half . . ."

Then there was a long silence within the room. The dog was barking. But the dog was not in that room. Was the dog out of the house? Cecil's toes began to feel for a hold upon the wall. He got himself higher and thrust his head and shoulders in.

The man was collapsed, arched backwards over the edge of the bed. Strange sounds were coming from his arched and naked throat.

Cecil thought, Sixty seconds would do it!

He couldn't afford *not* to take the risk. Could he?

Must be inside the car, she thought. Inside the car, then. Or in the trunk of the car.

It was so silent here. The sun was shining. She could see right through the car, the way it was tilted, to the other side of it. There was a shoe down there but there wasn't any foot in the shoe.

It struck her that this was a beautiful place. What a mad thought! She lifted her eyes and saw the wild hills. She turned her head and saw the colonnades of the pale bark-less tree trunks. She could see, down a kind of allée, that there was a house, way off, and a sound. The sound had made her turn her head. On the stoop of the old house there was the figure of a woman dressed in black, and beside her there was a big black dog. The woman looked like a witch.

Anabel got to her feet. She knew that, in the back of her mind, a lot of things were adding up, like a column of fig-. ures in plain arithmetic. But she didn't know what any of the items were.

Yes, *one*. Cecil Wahl had lied to her. He said he had seen. But he couldn't have seen. Because Anabel could not see. But how cruel!

Then there was the remnant of the uproar of the adrena-lin or whatever . . . the aftermath of her shock, when the grocery boy had made her think for a moment that Pat was alive. And there was something . . . And there was something . . . Idea in somebody's head that wasn't *so*.

Suddenly, her temper flared. Anabel began to take strides toward that house. Cecil Wahl wasn't visible. The two cars stood at the end of the road. She could see them.

Something was wrong with the picture.

Something was wrong with the whole setup. There was an idea in somebody's head that was not *so*.

Then she saw the woman duck back into her house, tak-ing the dog with her. She saw it. The furtiveness of it. Peo-ple lying to Anabel, hiding from her. . . .

Anabel was getting good and mad.

She began to run. She ran through the grove and through the gap in the fence where the gate hung crooked. She ran up on the stoop and she knocked, imperiously, at the door. The dog was barking furiously inside. Anabel was not afraid of dogs.

She saw a mad old face, bobbing at the window. Anabel didn't care that it was mad. "Let me in," she cried. "I want to *know*. Is Mr. Wahl in there?"

Mr. Wahl was climbing in at the bedroom window.

The old woman was muttering, undertone to the dog's noise. Anabel didn't care what she was muttering. She kept on knocking, hard and loud. She kept on calling, "Let me in." She pushed. She couldn't *wait!*

The door opened. There was the old woman and the big black fierce dog, held at his collar not as much by her old hand as by her old authority.

"I am Anabel—"

"You are not," cut in the old woman ferociously. "He don't mean anything by that. He don't mean a thing in the world. So you git! You hear? You, girl? None of *you*. You don't bother me."

The dog was turning and twisting as if he, too, were mad. Or of two minds. As if there was more than one alien thing against which he must defend his mistress.

Where? Beyond that closed door, directly across this room? (The old witch has got him.)

Anabel said, "The police are coming."

"None of them," screeched the old woman. The dog's frenzy now turned her body. Anabel saw the back of her dress.

"You had better tell me," cried Anabel. "*Who* doesn't mean anything? By *what? Where is he?*"

"I'll set the dog on you!" the old woman shrieked. "Or anybody else. *Nobody* bothers me."

But Anabel said, "Me, either."

Her long legs scissored across the room, past the old woman and the struggling straining snarling beast, straight to the door that was closed.

Anabel opened it. The inner room was dimmer. But there were people. Anabel stepped out of the way of what light she had let in, through the door, and she saw a pair of hands. A pair of hands. In the air. Held out—fingers tensed —in the air.

Behind her the old woman screamed, "Get 'em, Rex. Eh, Rex? Get 'em! Get 'em!"

And the black dog came like a bullet, hit the door. The door whanged all the way open, to slam upon the wall.

Maclaren steered around the corner into Oleander Street. He had slowed, to take the turn. Suddenly there was a figure, semaphoring at the side of the road, beside a panel truck.

"Hey! Hey!" Stan yelled. (The police had told him that the police were coming. He recognized the *girl!*)

Maclaren braked and Carlson leaned.

"He's in the witch's house," Stan yelled. "O'Shea. O'Shea. And she's crazy and watch the dog!"

Maclaren tramped on the accelerator. His body was very solid, as Vee could sense. Carlson calmly loosened his jacket. He had a gun under there. His body was solid. Their calm was very solid. So was their competence. Maclaren was driving very fast, but carefully, too. He hit the horn. The car bounded upon the twisting road.

Vee's heart was up. It was thrilling! But this was the way

they *did*. They did what was to be done. Solidly, calmly, fast and sure.

She wanted to cry. She wanted to laugh.

They spun to a stop where the Olds was, and Mrs. Newcomb's car. "Cecil?" gasped Vee.

Carlson said to her, "Stay," as if she were a dog.

The two of them then, policemen, shoulder to shoulder, their guns ready, ran for the trouble, ran up on the stoop of the bungalow, because from inside there was the noise of screaming, the sound of violence.

Vee stayed in the car and said out loud, "Oh yes! Oh yes!" and couldn't have told what she meant.

Carlson hit the door. The first room was empty. The old woman was standing square in the bedroom door. She was screaming. She had a staff in her hand and it was raised high. She was going to whack something or somebody. Somebody on the bed.

Maclaren got the staff in his left hand and took it and the old woman to one side.

Carlson could see a man and a dog threshing on the dusty rug in there. The shade had been torn from the window, giving light to see by. Something had been broken. They threshed over broken glass. There was blood and the man was screaming. The dog was going to kill him, if once the dog could shift his jaws from the forearm, just at the shoulder, to the throat.

Carlson was quick and smart. He fell prone upon the floor, gun in hand, got the gun under the dog and fired upward.

The dog died without making too much fuss about it.

The man screamed, "Get him off me! Get him off!"

Carlson went on his knees to try to loosen the dead jaws. "Take it easy," he said to the white face and the green eyes of Cecil Wahl.

Carlson jumped about six inches when there was a *thunk* behind him. He looked and the dog was not twitching. The old woman had plunked her bones down upon the floor beside the dog's carcass.

Maclaren was lifting, with gentle hands, the bare legs of a man up upon the mattress. Anabel O'Shea was lying across the bed, holding the man with one arm over his chest and one over his thighs, holding him up and away from the late violence as best she could, leaving her back vulnerable to the old woman's staff. The blow had not fallen. Anabel forgot about it.

She sat up and took the man's head against her breast. "He is burning," she said clearly and calmly in the sudden silence. "Get the doctor. Call. Find the phone."

The man was unshaven; he was a very sick man; he looked as if he were dying. But he opened his eyes and croaked reproachfully, "I would have called you."

"Don't you think I know that?" said Anabel, and her voice was so . . . so . . . something, Carlson's young eyes stung.

She said, "Will you get some help please? Will you hurry?"

Carlson looked down at the man on the floor, who was lying in the posture of the Dying Gladiator, heaving at the chest.

Maclaren said, "I'll watch it."

So Carlson stepped over the dead dog and around the old woman, who was stroking the dog's fur and muttering.

"Good dog. Eh, Rex? Be fine. You'll see." Or something like that.

Carlson tore out to the car and grabbed the telephone. "O'Shea's alive in there," he told Vee. "Cecil Wahl's been bit."

Stan Simmons was standing at the other side, looking in. "Oh, my gosh," he was saying. "Oh, my gosh, why didn't you ask me? I saw him. Jamie, he saw both of them."

"Went out on that already," the voice said on the phone. "Ambulance to the end of Oleander. Ought to be there in half a second."

So Carlson asked for more men, more help.

"Hey Carlson"—the voice held him—"what do you know? Adams chickened out on the suicide deal. They found him—where you said."

Carlson put up the phone.

Stan said, "Listen, I *told* them there was a sick man out here in the witch's house. O'Shea, I told them."

Vee hissed at him. "*Sssh.*" She said to Carlson, "I heard. You *go.*" Because she understood.

Carlson went racing back into the bungalow.

Cecil Wahl was sitting on the straight chair now, his jacket and shirt pulled away from his wounds. He was saying to Maclaren, "I thought I could get him out of the house, away from the dog. I might have done it if *she* hadn't come flying in like that, letting the damn dog in."

He glanced nervously and resentfully at Anabel.

She wasn't listening. She was touching her husband's face in certain small caresses, sending as best she could her life to him.

Cecil got up. "I can drive. My sister's in the hospital. I think . . ."

"Your sister is dead," said Carlson. "She jumped from the fourth floor."

Maclaren looked quickly at Carlson, who was having no pity, to whom this Cecil was beginning to smell.

Cecil's green eyes winced, briefly. "Oh, no! Poor C." But the cold eyes slanted to glance at the unshaven dirty haggard unconscious face of Pat O'Shea, a pitiful sight on Anabel's breast. "Will he live?" asked Cecil.

Nobody answered. Cecil glanced at Carlson. He held out his hand. "I guess you saved my life, pal," he said heartily, "corny though it sounds." (One young buck to another.)

But Carlson did not take the offered hand. He said, "Don't you care why?"

"Why?" Eyebrow went up.

"Why your sister jumped?"

"Oh, well . . ." Cecil swayed. "Her husband . . ."

"You think so?" said Carlson.

"Best I get out from underfoot," said Cecil. "You've got your hands full here." He staggered; he was trying to be charming.

"Better wait on a doctor," said Maclaren, mildly. "And there'll be a few questions."

Cecil took a step. Carlson snapped, "You heard the Lieutenant. And by the way, your sister's husband isn't dead. They've got *him*."

Cecil's face went very still. He was hunched protectively over his own wounds. Now he swayed and went down. Suddenly, he was sitting on the floor. His right hand began to grope. It found the thin shards from the lamp chimney. It took Carlson a moment or two to realize that the man was busily and deliberately mutilating his own fingertips.

When he saw it, he stopped it; there was noise outside. Ambulance. Then a police car. Then another. People.

They took O'Shea. They took the old woman. They took the dog's body.

Carlson stood beside Cecil Wahl. Maclaren said, "How did you know O'Shea was in there? Why did you have your hands on his throat? What was the idea?"

"Not I," said Cecil. "Not I."

"I saw," said Maclaren quietly, "the red marks of your ten fingers. Nobody else was in this room."

"He's got fingers," snapped Cecil. "O'Shea has."

"Only five," said Maclaren.

After that, Cecil would not speak. They took him away. They took Vee Adams back to town; a uniformed man drove her in Mrs. King's Oldsmobile.

Because nobody—not all the converging agents of law, order and mercy, separately or together—had been able to take Mr. O'Shea anywhere without also taking Mrs. O'Shea.

Friday Evening

VEE ADAMS was sitting with Carlson in his car. Mrs. King was awfully nice, but they wanted to talk. About Carlson, who had always had a desire to get into police work, although he'd never said too much about the way he felt to anyone before. People don't always understand.

About Vee, who was moving into the dormitory tomorrow. The Provost had fixed it, for the rest of the term. After that, it depended, some, on where and how her father was.

"I guess you saw your father, did you, Violet?"

"This afternoon. He doesn't seem to know what's happened. It was awfully hard to talk to him at all."

"I'll bet."

"You know, Beau, I don't feel as if I ever really, in my whole life, knew him. Not himself. My own mother, well . . . she always wanted things to be nice. Maybe it wasn't fair. I could have been nicer *to* him."

"Kids," said Carlson, "get impressions. I guess they have to be too . . . well, you know . . . too simple? I had a stepfather."

"Did you?" She turned to him in sympathy and wonder.

"We got along fine. He died last year. See, my Mom divorced my real father when I was six years old. She's been dead three years."

"We're both kind of orphans then," Vee said. "My father's alive, of course."

"So is mine," said Carlson. "It's not generally known."

He fell silent but she knew there was something else he wanted to tell her.

"Beau? Oh, I'm sorry. I keep using that old nickname because . . . I just don't even know your real name."

"My real name is James Maclaren," said Beau Carlson, tasting it.

The Provost couldn't do a thing with Mr. and Mrs. O'Shea. He wanted to discuss the whole affair with maturity, compassion, mercy, and understanding. They wouldn't even be serious.

As far as the theft was concerned, he had told them, the University would no doubt recover the cost, and, after all, the poor woman was dead. The poor man—pitiable.

"Pity me?" said Pat. He was clean-shaven and there was a neat piece of tape over the healing cut on his scalp. His right leg was strung up in one of the intricate contraptions that a hospital provides. His right arm lay quiet, but Anabel was tucked under his good left arm. Up on the hospital bed, she was—committed not to jiggle, but with her ankles crossed insouciantly, and looking very pleased to be there, not caring who knew it.

"He clobbered you, good," said she.

"Well actually, what he did, he hit me in the head."

"Stole the car."

"Stole the money. You always forget the money, Anabel."

"How much?" she asked shrewdly.

"Oh, just the two or three hundred I usually carry—for tips, you know."

"Then he goes and casts our perfectly good car off the mountain."

"Had that dent in the right front fender. Needed a lube, too. Still . . ."

"Stole your raincoat. Only six years old."

"And my hat, don't forget. A dollar eighty-nine."

"A dollar ninety-eight," cried Anabel.

The Provost sighed. He knew all the anguish they were leaving out. They were good kids.

"She argues, all the time," Pat told the Provost happily, "but she sure smells good. So do I. *I* feel like a blooming rose. I tell you, there's nothing like a hospital."

"For fainting?" said Anabel.

"Well, it ain't hay."

The Provost was absolutely lost, not being an "Alice" fan.

Maclaren put his head in. "Dropped by to see how you are doing. Mrs. O'Shea. Mr. O'Shea. Mr. Drinkwater."

The Provost said he was just leaving. He thought he might as well. O'Shea was, no doubt, still a little feverish, and his wife giddy with relief. He could forgive them. As he went out, he heard Pat say loudly, "Hey, Lieutenant, how can we railroad Adams into some cushy hospital? Do we do a deal? Who do we have to bribe?"

"Whom," said Anabel.

The Provost was halfway down in the elevator before

he realized that there already had been compassion, mercy, and understanding. It would be only a nine days' wonder, then.

He braced himself. The press was downstairs. Well. His school was a good school, a great school. Those young people, up there, were good young people. The Adams girl was a good kid. There were thousands of good kids on his campus. Many fine teachers. None of them were going to be hurt if he could help it. *He'd* deal with the press. He had his skills.

"Hey," said Pat joyously. "We have here none other than the Answer Man. Where's our list, Anabel?"

Maclaren said he had just retired, as of one hour.

"Never mind. Sit down. There are a few little points. I'm not going to ask you why Celia Adams did the Dutch and Everett didn't."

"I spent some time with him today. He doesn't know." Maclaren's beautiful voice was kind.

"*Was* Celia Adams mixed up in an old murder?"

"We don't know."

"*Yet*, you mean. O.K. Why did my car go off the mountain?"

"We don't—"

"Yeah. Yeah. But what does Adams say?"

"As near as I can figure, he skidded. Rear wheels were on the edge. He got scared, for a guess—afraid that somebody *would* stop to help him. Don't know, really."

"This is proceeding famously," said Pat. "Eh, what? Why was my wallet mailed in Barstow?"

"We don't know," said Maclaren flatly.

"Somebody put it in a mailbox," said Anabel, mischievously. "I'll *bet* that's it."

"It's a theory." Maclaren grinned at her fondly. "Maybe Adams dropped it on the bus. Somebody kicked it off in Barstow."

"And we'll never know," said Pat. "O.K. Why the dickens was Cecil Wahl out at the end of Oleander on Thursday morning?"

"Or in the night before?" chimed Anabel. "Jamie saw him. That's the 'chicken' boy. I drove Mother and Sue out there today and talked to him. Had to make it clear that *I* was married to the 'nice man.'"

"Anabel," said Pat, "kindly stop yakking?"

But Maclaren was shaking his head. "We don't know why Cecil was out there. He's not talking."

"He was mixed up in the murder with his sister, wasn't he?" demanded Anabel.

"We don't know," said Maclaren. "But we will probably find that out. We're hanging on to him. How is your throat?"

"Fine. Fine. He didn't have time to get set, really, before Anabel let the dog in."

"Nobody needs to kid me," said Anabel cheerfully. "I let Cecil in. Well, didn't I? Something I said. Then I went off and gave him his chance." She didn't sound too upset.

"You never know, sweetheart," said Pat soothingly. Then to Maclaren, "He messed up his fingerprints. A guilty conscience?"

"Well, they're not the only kind of evidence in the world," said Maclaren comfortably.

"Anyhow, you've got them now," said Anabel.

Maclaren said, "Wait a minute. We have?"

"Don't you *know?*" Anabel laughed with delight. "Well, let me tell you. Cecil bought a box of chocolate-covered cookies. He left them in the store. Stan gave them to Jamie. Jamie conked out all day yesterday; he was pooped. So nobody ate them. Well, Cecil had touched one and there it was. Now of course," she continued, looking wise, "that may not stand up as evidence in court, but it *is* a clue."

"Who told you this, Mrs. O'Shea?"

"Why your . . . I don't know his first name. Carlson."

"James," said Maclaren, his kind ugly face suffused with a foolish tenderness.

"He was out on Oleander Street, being a regular beaver," Anabel told him.

Pat said suddenly, "How is the old lady?"

"She can't live alone."

"No more?" said Pat sadly.

"She won't be kicked around. She's still saying he isn't dead."

"Johnny Pryde?"

"Yes—but I meant the dog."

"Poor soul," said Pat. "One rotten son."

"And that was the end of her," said Anabel. (She would feel pity some other day.) "Wow, but I'm lucky. Or else, smart."

"Lucky is what *you* are," said Pat severely. "A fifty percent chance that dog would have jumped you."

"A thirty-three and a third percent chance," said Anabel indulgently, and then to Maclaren, "He teaches math, you know."

Maclaren was laughing, when Miss More put her

starched head in. "Visiting hours are over," she caroled. Then shocked, "Mrs. *O'Shea! Not* on the *bed!*"

Anabel reversed the position of her ankles delicately. "How kind of you to come and tell us," she caroled dangerously.

Maclaren was a man who knew when a rule needed breaking and a lie needed telling. "I'm from the police. I wonder . . ." He took the starched one firmly away.